SECOND CHANCE HERO

Meet bad boy pitcher, Zach Pritchett...

Two things I love: baseball and Lacey Stark. Back in college, I had them both. But after graduation, I made the biggest mistake of my life. I let Lacey go.

Five years later, I can't complain. A Cy Young winner, I've achieved what I set out to do—pitching in the Major Leagues. Life is great.

Until it's not.

And the day it all went south? The day Lacey Stark appeared at my post press conference. The reality of not having her slams against my chest. Lacey's still sexy as hell, sporting more curves and a little more sass. Pitching in the Majors isn't the only thing I want anymore. Now, it's time to go after what I've denied myself all these years. I want Lacey and will stop at nothing until I make her mine.

Lacey seems determined to stay away, but we belong together. I know this. I just need to convince her to give me another chance.

Because one thing is guaranteed, I won't stop until she's back in my arms.

SECOND CHANCE HERO

Bad Boys Redemption: Book One

KIMBERLY READNOUR

Rae-Allen Publishing

ASIN: B074DLCBW6

ISBN: 978-1976074387

Cover Design by Daqri Bernado of Covers by Combs

Editing by Kelly Hartigan (XterraWeb) editing.xterraweb.com

Printed by Createspace

❀ Created with Vellum

To all fans of Baseball and Romance.

AUTHOR NOTE

Baseball! Oh, how I love the game. There are a few things I need to clarify in case you read this and scratch your head, thinking, "Hey wait a minute."

In order for the storyline to work, I had to adjust the College World Series timeframe. Normally, the wonderful series lasts through June, but that wasn't going to work for me. So what could I do? Well, I pulled out the fiction card and cheated. I ended the season during graduation. Please, please, please forgive me. During the time of writing, I just couldn't see any other way around it. Hopefully, it doesn't throw you off too badly.

UNFORESEEN LOVE: THE NOVELLA OFFER

Pick up your FREE novella today for joining my newsletter, and be among the first to learn about my new releases and giveaways. Find out more after you read Second Chance Hero.

CHAPTER ONE

LACEY

CITI FIELD STADIUM

ZACH PRITCHETT. THE ONE NAME I NEVER WANT TO SEE ON MY itinerary. *Ever*. But I'm not stupid and know the possibility of our paths crossing exists. I just refused to believe they ever would. I don't care that the position I accepted places me in press conferences with professional athletes. There are one hundred and sixty-two regular season games. With a five-man pitching rotation, the probability of being in the same room with him is rather low. But as today proves, my odds are not favorable. Then again, when have they ever been when it comes to that man?

I close my eyes and try concentrating on the surrounding chatter. The buzz of well-acquainted sports journalists—the deep masculine chuckles and feminine laughs from people comfortable being here—fills my ears.

I'm so jealous.

Although, I shouldn't be. I've put in as much, if not more, legwork as any other person in this room. I've earned my spot to be here.

As far as Zach goes? I'm seated in the fourth row toward the

1

edge and highly doubt he'll see me. Of course, I could shrink farther in my seat and hide behind the row in front of me. No matter what I do, I'll still be nervous.

God, five years have passed, and my heart still can't handle facing Zach. No way am I prepared to talk to him.

"Excuse me," a masculine voice says.

A young, dark-haired gentleman with eyes the color of a mocha latte stands to my right. I'd place him around my age of twenty-seven.

"Sure." I shift my legs to let him pass and try to pretend being here doesn't freak me out.

Mocha Latte Eyes sits next to me and opens his briefcase. As he rifles through his belongings, I continue to stare straight ahead and act casual. But it's almost time to start. Any second, I'll be in the same room with the guy who shattered my heart.

Tiny sweat beads form on my forehead, and I casually raise my hand and dab with my fingers to soak up the evidence.

Sweet Jesus. I'm totally freaking out.

Dangerous thoughts infiltrate my mind. Stupid ones like what if Zach notices me and shows no signs of regret? Or worse yet, doesn't recognize me. Or remember what we shared. I mean, my body has changed. I'm no longer that perky, slim college girl he let go. I'm not sure my fragile ego could withstand him passing over me. No matter how much I hate him.

The ball in the pit of my stomach tightens as I straighten my back. I'm so not ready to face him. Why, of all the assignments my boss gave me, do I get stuck in the same room as my ex?

New plan. Let everyone else ask the questions while I absorb the answers.

And believe me, there will be plenty of material to sort through with all questions directed toward Zach. After all, he swept into town and pitched a no-hitter against my beloved team, the Mets.

Asshole.

The man can pitch. Always could. Even in college. And what's worse, his success proves we made the right choice to end things.

That *he* made the right choice. I never agreed to end anything, but I didn't fight to keep him either. Although, I tried once. Three months after he left me, I went to see him. A sharp pain slices through my chest at that memory.

Damn it. I'm not strong enough for this.

"Are you new to the *Times*?" Mr. Mocha Latte Eyes asks.

Jesus, girl. Quit comparing this guy to a latte. I must be in dire need of coffee. Or something stronger to relax my nerves.

"Not exactly, but this is my first assignment."

I've been with the *New York Times* for almost five years now. It's taken me awhile to get to the sports journalist position, and even though it wasn't what I had intended to do, I'm grateful for this opportunity. But I'll keep that information locked tight. No stranger needs to know my life story. No one does.

"I'm Brayden Hicks with CBS New York."

He extends his hand, and when I shake it, his hand is warm and soft. Not at all like the callused ones I prefer. Like pitcher's hands.

"Lacey. Lacey Stark. Pleased to meet you."

"Pleasure's mine. If you need anything, I'm here to help."

"Thanks. I'll keep that in mind." I end with a warm smile and turn my attention to the front. Brayden seems nice, but I can't focus on any other guy right now.

"Okay, we'll have the coach answer a few questions, then open it up for the one you're all waiting for, Zach Pritchett," the media relations guy announces.

Brayden doesn't say anything else and faces forward himself. My stomach churns. This interview will not be good.

I swallow my insecurity and watch as Coach McFay steps to the platform. A moment later, the blond-headed star pitcher waltzes in behind with his confident swagger. He always was a cocky bastard. That hasn't seemed to change.

As Zach extends his arms to pull the chair out, his white shirt sleeves fit snug against those massive biceps. His six-foot-three-inch frame settles into the seat, and I can't help but gawk. Damn, he's filled out nicely since the last time I saw him. All lean muscle, he looks good. All hints of boyish features are long gone, replaced by a strong, chiseled jaw masked with stubble. He never did shave on the days he started.

I bite my nail as my focus shifts to his perfectly thinned lips. Oh, those lips that dominated every kiss. Spearmint floods my senses from the memory of that perfection, his greedy tongue claiming me. He always tasted of spearmint. Does he still?

No. No. No. I will not allow my thoughts to stray there. Zach Pritchett crushed me when he left, and I never fully recovered. I will *not* revisit that memory.

"What was the morale of the dugout?"

"At what part did you let the no-no enter your mind?"

Questions are flung at Zach, but he answers each one with the grace of a seasoned player. I'm not surprised; he's always been good at everything he does.

Zach smiles and brings his large fingers to his chin. My body betrays me as my nipples harden and press against my bra, yearning for those big hands to caress my skin. Among other things. He sure could fuck. He brought my orgasms to a whole other level, and no one since has matched his skill. Or even come close.

That pisses me off more.

"What does the last out of a no-hitter feel like?"

To hell with these bullshit questions. How do you think Zach felt? He felt freaking fantastic. I need a question that gets to the heart of the matter. I'm sorry, Mr. Pritchett, but I know exactly what to ask. Your physical appearance and performance may have improved, but you haven't shed your little habit. And I'll be the one to call you out on it.

"Mr. Pritchett," I shout. "Do you expect the pain in your left shoulder to be a lingering problem?"

Zach's head snaps toward mine, our gazes locking.

Warmth travels through my bloodstream and heats places that haven't been alive in months. *Crap.* I think I just messed up.

CHAPTER TWO

ZACH

FIVE YEARS AGO

HOURS AFTER THE GAME, ADRENALINE STILL PULSES THROUGH MY veins. I pitched through the eighth and brought Penn State the win. I'm pumped.

Thank God, the ice down helped my pitching shoulder. It feels great, which is good. I don't have time for nagging problems. This is my last year to pitch at the collegiate level, and if I'm going pro and pushing for the contract my agent insists I can get, I must be in top shape. There's no room for injuries.

"Great game," Derek says, shoving a beer in my hands. "The team's looking good."

"Yeah, I like our chances." I sip the lukewarm beer, more out of politeness than anything. I don't drink much during ball season. Derek wouldn't know minor details about me though. He's in my business law class and part of this fraternity. It's not as if we hang around each other all the time. Truth be known, I think he befriended me in hopes to score with the cleat chasers. I give my standard go-to answer whenever people tell me how the team looks. "We have a good chance at making the playoffs."

It's early in the season, but the team's in great shape. We have a group of talented guys, and we're in it to win this year.

A skinny brunette in a tight V-cut black dress stares at me from across the living room. She positions herself—in what I can only presume is a practiced maneuver—to reveal half of her too-large-to-be-real tits. When she flashes me a smile, I ignore her. Any other night, I'd be all into that, but I'm more intrigued by the couple in the background. Well, only one of them in particular.

Lacey Stark.

The girl I like to refer to as the sexy redhead. She was on the baseball field the other day, and yeah, I may have asked about her. Something about the way her auburn curls glowed in the setting sun caught my attention. Well, that and the way her black jeggings showcased those muscular legs. I do love legs that are fit. But I've heard how passionate redheads can be in the sack. So, can you blame a guy for being curious?

Lacey's part of the communication department, and my team-mate Jax Carrigan shares a class with her. He crushed all hopes of a quick hookup when he said the two devastating words—not single. She's dating an asshole by the name of Jason Kerr—a spoon-fed frat boy. I'm not giving up on her, though. I'll wait for a better opportunity. But watching the way her boyfriend's hands flail about, I'm seconds away from creating that chance.

The brunette ignores my non-interested hint and saunters over to Derek and me. This seems to perk Derek up until she wraps her arms around my waist.

"You looked great out there today, Zach." She flutters her eyelids and half-grins.

I'm not going to lie; her tight little body pressed against mine —fake or not—feels good, but not good enough to hold my atten-tion. Lacey's boyfriend is getting angrier as he talks. I swear, if he lays a hand on her, I'll pummel him, hurt shoulder or not.

"Thanks. You go to every game?" I direct my question to the girl hanging off me but maintain focus on Lacey. I don't need to listen to the brunette; the sad reality of her "yes" answer is inevitable. Cleat chasers go to all the games with high hopes of scoring with a player. I often wonder if it matters which guy they land. Hell, I'm not innocent. I've nailed a girl or two that's made her way around the baseball carousel, but I'm not proud.

As the chick answers, Lacey's boyfriend backs down, and I relax a bit. Maybe too much because my attention shifts to Lacey's mouth. Her bottom lip is plumper than the top, and I conjure an image of those lips wrapped around my cock. I bet she feels fantastic.

Lacey places her hands on her hips and glares at her boyfriend. A thrill surges through me. Damn, I want those fiery eyes staring at me. Her look alone is a turn-on. Between those lips and her stance, the need to adjust my pants presents itself. I don't dare do it though. Not with this girl attached to my side. Now isn't the time for mixed signals.

Lacey opens her mouth, but she speaks too low to overhear. Like a stalker, I keep watching. Her lips are easy enough to read as she mouths "Not here."

The Asshole's voice rings loud, but the words are certainly not clear. It appears Mr. Ass has had too much to drink. With a quick huff, Lacey looks away. After a beat, she scans the room but stops when she lands on me. Her entire body stills, but I can't read her stonewalled expression. Surprise? Interest? Disgust? I'm not sure.

She blinks out of her trance and glances at the girl who's staking claim to my waist. I really need to find a gentle way to ditch this girl.

With a quick shake of her head, Lacey shifts her focus back to her boyfriend. A moment later, she flinches at whatever the jerk says before he stalks away. As Lacey huffs out a breath, I suppress a grin at my good fortune. The opportunity to talk to her came quicker than anticipated.

Not wasting any time, I untangle myself from the brunette's clutches. "Have you met Derek?"

He perks up when I steer her toward him. *This is your moment,*

Derek, don't strike out. With a pat on the back, I wink. "Catch you later."

There. He's happy. She's...shit. She's glaring at me. Definitely not happy. I tamp down the guilt, because face it, who would be using who here? I pop a stick of gum in my mouth and then chew super fast. Nothing is worse than stale beer breath when you're trying to impress the chicks.

I trek toward Lacey, totally not checking out how great the material stretches across her tight little ass. My hands stay planted by my side, safe and sound. It's not in my nature to grab a girl without permission, but man, the temptation is strong.

"So, why are you standing over here by yourself?" I ask.

Lacey's body stiffens before turning around. She throws a nervous glance to where her boyfriend has disappeared before refocusing her attention to me.

"I'm waiting on my friend Jocelyn."

"Hmm, friend? Not boyfriend?"

"Uh ... yeah, him too."

The hint of coolness in her tone intrigues me, and I jump at the opening.

"I can't help but wonder," I ask, letting my words linger, baiting her.

She cocks her head and studies me for a moment before she bites. "Wonder what?"

Caution rings in her tone, but I hold back my smile.

"Why he'd leave you alone in the first place?"

"Stalk much?"

Her eyes flare, and this time, I don't even try stopping my smirk. It's almost too easy getting her riled.

"Couldn't help seeing your argument."

"That's not your concern. Is it?" Her chin juts upward as if she's tough and ready to challenge me, but she can't hide her flushed cheeks.

Her attitude along with the tiny freckles splayed across the base of her nose distract me. She's too freaking cute. The assurance etched in her expression is so damn hot I'm sure the moral center of my brain threatens to shut down as I'm picturing her lying naked beneath me, releasing that pent-up frustration. Damn, this girl's getting to me.

"No. But I think it could be." I step closer but leave a small gap between us. Her breath hitches and then accelerates, and her slight discomfort from my closeness causes a thrill to pulsate through me. She's interested in me whether she wants to be or not.

"Are you sure about that? I think your girlfriend is shooting mental daggers at me." She nudges her chin toward the area I just left.

Damn, Derek must've struck out already. He's nowhere to be found. The brunette, though? She stands with her arms crossed, scowling at us. Well, those laser-beamed daggers point more toward Lacey than me. I shoot an apologetic glance at the girl, but that seems to piss her off more.

"She's not my girlfriend."

"You looked rather cozy a few minutes ago." The little challenge to her voice is too tempting to ignore.

"Jealous?"

"What? No! I have ... a boyfriend." She drops her head, a soft red tint coloring her porcelain skin.

"You mean the jerk who left you alone?"

She shrugs. "Good game today, by the way."

"You watched?" I don't bother with hiding my surprise. Her commenting on my performance is the last thing I expect.

"Wouldn't make a good sports communication student if I didn't watch the games. Now would I?"

I stare down at her in awe. *Shit*. She may be my dream girl.

"But I'm concerned about your shoulder," she adds.

And just like that, she douses every hot amber flaming inside of me with a bucket of ice water. I think my balls shriveled up and ran inside. I stay quiet and eye her for a moment. "Why do you say that?"

"The little tic you do right before you get ready to pitch. It seems you're favoring your left shoulder. I figured it must be hurting."

What the fuck? How did she notice that? Before my windup, I tug my shoulder down for a stretch. The movement is so slight I never dreamt anyone would see. Or figure out the reason behind me doing it.

"I'm fine. It's just an old habit I can't seem to shake," I lie. "How did you even know?"

"I've been watching you since the season started."

Her admission brings forth a foreign sensation that invades the pit of my stomach. A sudden warmth attacks my body like a parasite burrowing in its host to get nutrition. It's a heat-generating leech playing havoc with my nervous system. I've never felt this way before, but I can admit one thing—my balls are officially thawed.

"I like you, Lacey Stark." The corner of my mouth draws up from the surprise in her widening eyes, and I refrain from planting a kiss on those cute little freckles. Closing the small gap between us, I move my mouth next to her ear. Her tits press against my chest. With our bodies pressed together, I hope she doesn't feel my semi her diamond-hard nipples caused. "That's right. I know your name, and one day soon, you'll be screaming mine while quivering beneath me."

Her small gasp is sexy as hell as I shoulder past her. *That's right, sweetheart. Think about that while you sleep tonight. You can bet your sweet ass I'll be thinking about you.*

CHAPTER THREE

LACEY

CURRENT DAY

UNCOMFORTABLE QUIETNESS LOOMS OVER THE CONFERENCE room as everyone awaits the answer that raised speculation. *Is the Cy Young Winner hurt?* Indifference masks Zach's initial surprise, and despite my heart fluttering faster than a hummingbird's wings, I relax somewhat. There's recognition behind his stare, and I can't believe how happy that makes me. I'm not supposed to have any feelings.

"No," he answers with assertion.

His denial is my cue to let the questionable pain situation go, but do I? Nope. Evidently, I like torturing myself.

"So, the pain is more temporary?" I ask.

A slight hint of anger flashes behind those deep blue eyes, but I don't care. I've had enough anger streaming through my veins for the last five years. Zach Pritchett's uncomfortableness for lying to his coaches, yet again, is the least of my worries.

Zach works his jaw back and forth, his gaze never straying from mine. We're in a stare down in front of the top sports journalists of New York City. I won't cave. I know I'm right.

"Yes," Zach admits after a beat.

Chatter breaks through the room followed by many questions. Indifference masks the initial shock on Zach's coach's face as he tries to downplay the situation. A hint of remorse filters in at smothering the high from pitching the no-hitter. And for what? A headline? Revenge? I'm not sure why I did it. Maybe part of me wanted to get back at him. Whatever the reason, guilt creeps into my conscience.

Coach McFay leans to his left and whispers to Zach. As Zach nods, he shifts back to me, and this time, he doesn't break eye contact. The air thickens, laced with sudden regret and lingering hate. It's so stifling I can hardly breathe.

"Good job, Lacey Stark. I'm impressed," Brayden says.

I murmur a thanks, but his admiration doesn't lessen the sting from my self-loathing. If anything, his praise deepens my guilt.

"How did you know?"

I peel my gaze from Zach and focus on the guy beside me. Brayden leans in as if I'm telling him a deep dark secret. I'm not admitting anything. That's Zach's secret to tell.

"I just knew," I say.

"Uh-huh. Okay then." The corners of his eyes crinkle as he laughs. "Impressive, at any rate."

Like a child to the concession stand, my gaze returns to Zach, and he continues to stare at me. Expressionless. He's also not answering any of the journalists' questions—his coach has that covered.

"And that's all I'll elaborate on." Coach McFay stands, prompting Zach to move.

A twinge of emptiness followed by a need to leave slices straight to my core. I lower my head and take a few calming breaths. *Calm down. The situation isn't that bad.* Yes, it is. I just revealed his pain in front of everyone. What was I thinking? This man could destroy the life I have built, and I practically welcomed him back into it.

In a rush to exit, I twist and rise too fast. The chair leg catches my foot, and I fall face-first into a hard wall of muscle. My eyes trace along defined pecs hidden beneath the buttoned collared shirt and continue their path upward until I meet those piercing blue eyes—the same ones that have haunted me since the day he walked out of my life.

Long, deft fingers wrap around my hips, and I want to curse my body because I ache for more of his touch. Our bodies pressed together, his breath on my face, it's all too much. I inhale a jagged breath but wish I hadn't. *Spearmint.* Jeez. Does he own stock in the gum company?

"Whoa, in a hurry to get away from me?"

Yes, I think but respond with "No. Why would I be in a hurry?"

The corner of his mouth draws into that sexy half-grin I remember all too well. I need to get away from him before I do something stupid like run my hands along his hard pecs. God, he feels incredible against me. Better than I remember. It was hard back in the day controlling myself around him, but now, it's taking every ounce of energy not to make a bigger fool of myself.

He backs up and guides me away from the chairs, his hands still on my hips. Why does his touch still ignite my body?

"Sorry, I'm done interviewing," Zach says to Brayden at his approach. "I'm just saying hello to an old friend."

Friend?

Why does that word sting? It shouldn't. That's what we are, right? Or, at least that is what he thinks we are. According to him, we parted on good terms. He doesn't know I discovered the truth that awful night when I almost made a fool of myself. He has no idea how he ripped my heart apart. Coming back to my senses, I step away from Zach's grip. *Quit falling into his trap!*

"No, I didn't need to ask you anything. I'm just giving Lacey my card." Brayden looks at me and extends his hand. "I was serious before. If you need anything, please call. I'm sure we'll be seeing a lot more of each other."

"Thanks, Brayden." I grab the business card from him. "I look forward to seeing you again."

Brayden nods with a wink before turning to leave, my stare lingering after him. I can't believe he was ballsy enough to hit on me in front of a professional ballplayer. Maybe I'm misreading the meaning behind the wink.

"Am I intruding?"

I turn back to Zach. His jaw hardens, and he appears somewhat irritated. Or jealous. But that makes little sense. We're only friends. Old acquaintances. He has no right to act jealous.

"Hardly. We just met." I rein in my tone. There's no need to be snippy. I doubt I'll ever talk to Zach after today. I bite back a sigh and change tactics. "Congratulations. You pitched a great game today."

"I did, didn't I?" That sexy-as-hell grin is back, and I have to remind myself yet again that I don't like Zach Pritchett. Not anymore.

"Glad to see you haven't lost your confidence."

He laughs, and then his expression turns serious.

"You look good, Lacey." His gaze dips and roams along my body, lingering on my chest a moment before returning to my face. "I'm a little surprised to see you as a journalist, though. I kept looking for you in every stadium. Thought for sure you'd be working in media relations."

He looked for me? And there it is. That tiny spark of hope followed by a deep burn in my chest. His confession is nothing more than a dangerous game of what ifs. I need to abort this conversation. Fast.

"I decided on a different career path after my internship."

He nods, and instead of being smart and walking away, I stay rooted in place. His sun-streaked, blond hair is kept shorter but with enough length to weave your fingers through. I press my hands against my legs to stop from finding out if his hair is as soft as I remember. *Shit, my thoughts are weak around this man.*

"Do you live close by?"

My gaze wanders back to those sapphire-rich eyes.

"Somewhat." I don't elaborate. No way in hell am I giving him

14

my address. It's a one-to two-hour commute on a good day, so I doubt there's any chance he'll stop by, but still. That's one risk I'm not willing to take.

Zach glances at his coach who looks less than thrilled to be kept waiting. I'm sure he wants an exact update from Zach about his shoulder's condition.

"I better go. I have some explaining to do, thanks to you."

Heat flames my cheeks as the regret resurfaces.

"Sorry about that. I do want you to take care of yourself. If your shoulder pain has flared up again—"

"I'm fine. But I'm glad you still care."

I suck in a breath and bite my tongue.

"Meet me later tonight. We're staying at the Grand Hyatt hotel. I'll be in the lounge waiting for you."

With a subtle shake of my head, I lower my chin, suddenly finding my black dress shoes interesting.

"Lacey, it's *great* seeing you. I'd like us to catch up for old time's sake. You may as well come." He grabs my left hand and runs his thumb across the top of my knuckles before resting on my naked, ringless finger. "You know I always get what I want. It's just a matter of time."

The gleam in his expression dries my mouth, and I want nothing more than to meet him. But I can't. I can't allow him back into my life. Not to catch up. Not for anything.

"I'll try," I say, my own words deceiving me.

He squeezes and then releases my hand. "I'll be waiting."

I watch as he exits the room. God, what have I gotten myself into? I'm in a daze the entire time I walk to my car, and the anxiety doesn't leave as I slide behind the wheel. Zach wants to meet me? Shit! I'm pissed there's a small part of me that wants to take him up on his offer. But that cannot happen. I must stay far away from Zach Pritchett. Too many things are at stake.

Like my heart.

The last time I saw him was late August after we graduated. My fingers grip the steering wheel tight as the memory sparks a pang of grief and insecurity. I tried to make one last effort at salvaging our relationship and flew down to Florida where he was playing in the minors. He never knew I was coming. For some stupid reason, I felt surprising him would be better. There was a surprise all right, just not the one I expected. And five years later, the memory from that night still stings.

The warm, Floridian breeze did little to calm the excitement and anticipation that swirled through me the moment I stepped outside the airport. I only had one destination—Zach's apartment. I shot off a text to my best friend Jocelyn announcing my arrival as I waited for the Uber driver.

Thanks to Jocelyn's clever detective work, I had obtained his address. Still to this day, I have no idea how she found it, and I want to ask, but she seems reluctant to talk about it.

Forty-five minutes later, I found myself at the end of the hallway, standing in front of his door, contemplating what to say. I was naive enough to think my presence alone would be enough.

Room 21A. The shiny brass letters stared back, confirming the number written on the piece of scrap paper crumpled in my hand.

I raised my hand to knock but froze when I heard voices growing louder. I stood there, trying to ignore the sudden flip my stomach took. A shrill feminine yelp carried through the door, and the remnants of my in-flight crackers...? Yeah, they threatened to join the party. The last thing I had expected was a girl in his room. I just gaped at the door and swallowed back the threatening wail.

When a hard thud crashed against the door, the foggy haze clouding my mind lifted, and I raced to the opened stairwell and ducked behind the corner. I should have kept going and escaped before Zach saw me. But I didn't. My body had other plans. Instead, I sagged against the wall and listened as their voices carried down the corridor.

"Zach, I don't mind waiting."

"I'm sorry, babe, but the team takes off tomorrow, and it's really not fair to you."

"I think you're worth the wait. Come on, you can't deny we're good together."

He chuckled. The son of a bitch chuckled. Three short months before then, he confessed his love through a tearful goodbye. Three months! And he had already moved on?

Pain ripped through my chest and sliced my heart into tiny fragments. I pressed my hand against my stomach, trying desperately not to vomit.

"I had fun, and if I didn't have to concentrate on baseball, we could no doubt have more fun. But I have to focus on my career."

Her whiny pout was suffocating, and when she asked for one last kiss, I couldn't take any more. I ran down the stairs. Away from that horrific scene. Away from him.

It wasn't long after that Zach was called to the majors, and I never tried contacting him again.

I turn and drive away from the downtown area, the tears falling of their own accord. The entire time we were together, I never once felt used. After hearing him let that girl down gently, I felt sick, knowing his time with me meant so little. I sigh and continue to my run-down, cozy townhouse where I plan to remain the rest of the evening. But as I drive away from the hustling traffic, his message replays in my mind. *I always get what I want.*

Yes. Yes, you do Zach. That's exactly what scares me.

CHAPTER FOUR

ZACH

FIVE YEARS AGO

I GLANCE AT MY PHONE AND GROAN. ONE HOUR UNTIL PRACTICE is all I have. Surely, that's enough time for what I need to do.

Video games and empty food wrappers lay scattered on the floor as I step into the living room of the four-bedroom apartment. My roommates are slobs. The downfall for sharing living space with Jax and the twins, Brian and Brad Martin. Being pressed for time, I ignore the compulsion to throw away their trash. I gave up trying to make them clean up after themselves last year. The effort was futile. They didn't listen and made fun of me instead.

The place is quiet, and I'd be lying if I said I wasn't relieved. The brothers are in class, but this is Jax's time to chill at home. Maybe I'll be lucky, and he'll be gone. It's not a big deal if he's around, but he'll disapprove of Lacey and me hooking up. He's been acting weird ever since I mentioned her name. I understand his concern, but what the fuck ever. There's something about her I like, and I'm taking full advantage of this opportunity. Sure, she's a challenge; not too many girls dismiss me. In fact, I can't remember the last time a female-bodied member turned me down. When you're a jock on campus, there's never a shortage of girls willing to do *anything* for you. You want your dick sucked? Done. A three-way? Not a problem. That's the way of life, but none of those girls ever excite me. Well, I was excited for the moment, just not thrilled for a particular girl. But Lacey keeps popping in my thoughts: those cute freckles, her fiery gleam and the way her breath hitched when I stepped closer. I know I affected her. So, wouldn't the bigger question be why *wouldn't* I see where this leads?

I holler for Jax, but silence greets me. Good, he's gone. I beeline to my bedroom and don't bother closing the door. With a quick toss of my backpack, I shed my top. My perfect toss into the hamper scores me two points. The rest of the house may be a mess, but my room stays clean. I can't live in filth.

I retrieve my phone from my jeans pocket and pull up Lacey's number I'd retrieved earlier today. An easy enough task considering the circumstances. My fingers can't fly across the screen fast enough.

Me: *Don't lie, you've been thinking about me, haven't you? I bet Zach Pritchett was your last thought before falling asleep.*

Lord knows, she was mine.

Lacey: *How did you get my number?*

I chuckle, half-relieved she texted back. But getting her number was simple. All I had to do was find her friend Jocelyn and flash my smile. That girl caved quicker than my ninety-five-mile per hour fastball. But my secret weapon had more to do with her willingness than anything.

Me: *You don't have loyal friends. Or maybe you do, and they know your BF is a douche.*
Lacey: *Don't hold back.*

Me: *I always speak the truth.*
Lacey: *In this case, you'd be right. He is a douche.*
Me: *See. I'm always right. But I'm glad you recognize it.*

I plop on the bed and wait for a response. After a few minutes, it becomes obvious she isn't going to add anything else. *Oh, no. I'm not done talking to you, Miss Lacey Stark.*

Me: *What happened?*
Lacey: *Why do you care?*
Me: *I always care about the woman I'm fucking.*
Lacey: *We're not fucking.*
Me: *YET. We're not fucking yet. But I still care.*
Lacey: *My God, are you always this presumptuous?*

You have no idea.

Me: *I go after what I want.*
Lacey: *Strike me off your want list.*
Me: *So, that's a yes?*
Lacey: *Yes to what?*
Me: *Yes to going out with me.*
Lacey: *Didn't know you asked.*
Me: *Well, I did.*

I wait again. Silence. I grab my baseball from my nightstand drawer and toss it in the air. I catch it and repeat the motions. More silence.

"Fuck!" This requires the big guns. I will have to take Lacey out on a real date. Excitement surges through my body. Dating is something I never do. Never really had to since I've suited up. Like I said, girls tend to be a bit easy when you're a star athlete. But this chick is different and definitely making me work for it. An unexpected smile crosses my face. Challenge accepted.

"What's wrong?" Jax asks as he steps into my room.

My eyes narrow as I contemplate what to tell him. Jax has a weird hang-up about chasing after girls who have boyfriends. Don't get me wrong, I totally agree. People's relationships should always be respected, but this scenario is different. In my mind, Lacey deserves better than that jerk she's with, and besides, they've already broken up. At least I think they have.

"Nothing. Just texting Lacey."

"Damn it, Zach. She has a boyfriend. I told you that."

"I'm pretty sure they're no longer a couple. Besides, he's an ass."

"If that's the case, then she's on the rebound and vulnerable. Don't fuck with her."

I purse my lips and study Jax's stance: crossed arms, pinched expression. Hmm. He's truly annoyed with me. *What the fuck?*

"Where's this coming from?"

"I know you. You're not the serious type." He shifts his weight and cocks his head. "She's a nice girl. I don't want to see her get hurt. Besides, you know who her best friend is."

Ah, the real reason.

"I don't want to fuck her best friend."

The red blotches covering his face should've been my warning to shut the fuck up. I'm tormenting a caged animal who will strike any second.

"You damn well better not fuck her best friend," he says between clenched teeth. "I told you, you can't ever be serious. Stay away from her."

"Maybe I've never been serious because I haven't found anyone to be serious with."

This is the problem with having the persona of a man-slut. People think I'll never settle down. As if I'm incapable. And now that I found a girl who holds my interest past the sexual encounter, no one believes I can be serious. Like my only intentions in life are one-night stands. Do they believe it's impossible to fall hard and fast for anyone? Because it sure sounds like they do. I call bullshit. I'm perfectly capable of falling hard for someone. Is Lacey Stark the right woman for me? Who the fuck knows? But Lacey's the only girl to spark a legitimate interest in my four years' attendance at Penn State, and I'd like to see where this leads.

I've been focused strictly on baseball, having no time for commitments, but I go after what I want, and now? I want Lacey Stark. No matter what Jax may think, Lacey will be mine.

"I'm actually taking this girl out on a date." *Or at least I will.*

Jax looks genuinely surprised. That sort of pisses me off.

"Fine. Just tread lightly, my friend. I don't want to see her get hurt."

"I don't plan on hurting her. I *am* interested in more than sex." I pause. Until now, sex had been the only thing on my mind, but that has changed. A date with Lacey intrigues me. "Besides, what about me? What if I'm the one who ends up hurt?"

"Whatever." Jax turns to walk out my door. "We have practice. Get off your lazy, love-struck ass and move."

"Fucker. I'm coming." I throw the baseball at him, but he ducks in time. The ball ricochets off the hallway wall, and I frown at the small divot. Guess we can kiss our deposit goodbye. Picking up my phone, I stare at the blank screen. Lacey's lack of response baffles me. *What is up with this chick?*

Me: *I'm still waiting for an answer.*

I slam the phone on the mattress, not a hundred percent sure she'll respond. I stand and grab my practice shirt from the closet when the ping slices through the silence. Three quick strides and I'm next to my bed, glancing at the display. I don't even need to open the message to read it.

Lacey: *In that case, no.*

Oh, sweetheart, I'm not going away that easily. Time for plan B.

CHAPTER FIVE

LACEY

CURRENT DAY

"Time will be the true indicator of truth behind Cy Young Winner Zach Pritchett's shoulder pain."

I place my elbows on top of the wooden desk and stare at the last line of my article. The regret swirling through me is overbearing. Maybe I shouldn't have called Zach out, but if he's having shoulder pain, then he shouldn't be pitching nine innings. *Yeah right.* What sane individual would leave a game when throwing a no-hitter?

But more gnaws at me than my keen reporter skills. I didn't meet Zach last night, and it shouldn't bother me. Except, it does. I must be insane. Heck, he's a professional ballplayer for crying out loud. He wouldn't want anything to do with an ex-flame. Someone he used the last few months of college. I'm sure he never gave it a second thought that I didn't show. So, why do I care?

It's just, seeing him yesterday has opened my memory bank. All the hurtful feelings from our last night together, along with the hate I've developed toward him, betrays me, taking a back seat to the good times we had. And we did have some good times. Great even.

We dated for about three months. If I think about the time span, it is relatively short compared to most people's relationships. But it never seemed short at the time. We fell hard for each other. Or, I fell hard for him, and if I'm honest with myself, it was the best three months during my entire four years of college.

The realization of our past relationship should've been a sign. Some sort of forewarning of impending memories. But I didn't heed the warning. I was still caught off guard with the direction my thoughts went last night. Zach Pritchett can invade my mind, front and center, as if no time has passed. I'm hopeless.

Even now, because I can't stop picturing his hands on my hips. His gesture may have been innocent—he was, after all, keeping my clumsy butt upright—but the craving my body yearns for is real. I feel like a fairy-tale princess. For the past five years, I lay dormant only to be awakened by Prince Charming's touch.

It's almost laughable, but boy, did I become alive. Sleeping last night was near impossible. Despite how hard I try to hate that man, I never truly succeed, which is why I allowed my imagination to go wild while in bed last night. I visualized his fingers tracing along my skin, gliding along my breasts until my nipples hardened, begging for his mouth. I squirm in my seat as warm chills race through my core. Sweet Jesus, I can't get turned on at work. It's been months since I've been with a man. This must be the reason behind my response to his simple touch.

"Great job discovering the injury. Not to mention how great the article is written," my boss, Larry James, says, pulling me out of my Zach-induced fantasy.

I close my eyes momentarily and cringe at his words. The guilt grows deeper. I turn to face Larry and plant a smile on my face. "Thanks. I'm just doing my job."

"It's a great find, and I want you to be on top of this injury. Which is why you're booked on a plane in three days to San Diego."

"What? Why? The Mets are playing the Cubs, not the Padres."

His eyes hold a mischievous sparkle, and I fight the threatening groan as a sickening feeling claws its way through my body.

"No-no, my dear. It's not the Mets playing them. It's the Phillies."

Oh, God.

"Why?" I whine again.

"This is your story. Pritchett is up to pitch in four days, and you'll be able to watch him. You can judge for yourself if he's hurt. I have your credentials in place. You're set to go." Larry pats my shoulder and lays a folder on top of my desk. The top paper slides out and reveals the hotel I'll be staying at for the night. The Manchester Grand Hyatt. Not too shabby.

"Why is Pritchett's pain news?"

Larry raises an eyebrow and gives me a knowing look.

"Yeah, yeah, I know. The Phillies 'Mr. Cy Young' is up for contract negotiations." I blow out a breath. "No one needs to tell me how devastating shoulder injuries can be."

Larry cocks his head and studies me for a moment. "I thought you'd be more thrilled."

"I am," I reply quickly. "It just threw me off. That's all."

"It won't be too hard being around Zach again, will it? I know you guys attended Penn State together, but is there more to you guys?"

"No." I rush my words, my voice cracking. "Nothing like that. There's nothing to worry about."

"Okay, then." Larry eyes me for a moment and then nods. "You're the best fit for the job. I expect a great article when you get back."

He turns and walks away. I let out another slow breath as his footsteps fade in the distance. Jesus, he has no clue what's at stake. I cannot let Zach into my life. I can't. That door needs to remain shut. And how on earth am I going to be able to leave on a whim? There are arrangements that need to be made. I would've thought my boss, of all people, would know this. He's been an integral part of my life ever since he landed me that intern job after graduation. Are all guys desensitized to the needs of women? Jeez.

I glance at the time and then back to the "to do" pile begging for attention. It's only two thirty. I'll finish a few things before giving Jocelyn a call to dial-in my favor. She'll probably rope me into watching her rambunctious kids so she and Carl can have another date night. I swear the married mother of three has more entertaining evenings than me.

"Lacey." Michelle, the main receptionist, pants as she carries a slim, rectangular box. "You have a package."

In all my five years working here, I've never once received a gift. I'm instantly warm. The room temperature feels as if it increased by ten degrees.

Michelle places the cardboard box upright on top of my desk. I stare for a moment, no need guessing who the gift is from. With a calming breath, I open the top middle desk drawer in search for the box cutter. *Why are the walls suddenly closing in on me?* It's only a freaking gift for Chrissake.

Michelle, known for her nosiness, stays by my side. I'd ask her to leave, but I kind of want her support. A small wince escapes. I'm being reduced to wimp status by a freaking box.

"Oh, what do you think it is?" she asks.

"I'm not sure." I swipe the box cutter across the top and open the flaps.

"There's a note." Michelle's eyes widen as she looks on.

I pull the white card stock out, positioning it so Michelle can't read it. My private affairs don't need spread all over the office. The writing is unrecognizable, but the words leave no doubt as to who the mystery gift giver is.

"I missed you last night, but I'll bet you missed me too, especially when you tossed and turned. I still want to talk. You owe me for outing me in front of millions of fans on national TV. I'll be in touch."

Asshole.

But his arrogance can't stop the stupid grin forming on my face. He did wait for me.

"Who's it from?"

I pull out the bottle of wine and read the label: Happy Valley Red. I'm speechless. How the hell was he able to send me a bottle of my favorite wine from Happy Valley Vineyard and Winery so fast?

"Ooh, you have to tell me."

Michelle sounds as if she's about ready to burst with excitement, but I'm not going there. Not yet, anyway.

"Just an old friend."

"Uh-huh. From the way you're grinning, I'd say he's more than an old friend."

She's fishing or figured it out. I gulp. I'm in deep trouble.

CHAPTER SIX

ZACH

FIVE YEARS AGO

THE SUN'S GLARE AGAINST THE HEPPER FITNESS CENTER'S windows makes it damn impossible to determine if Lacey's inside working out. Of course, I don't think it's possible to see clearly at any given time. I'm just impatient. She should be done and ready to walk through the exit at any minute. That is if I have her schedule right.

I push the stalking feelings aside and lean against a small maple tree thirty feet away from the door. There isn't much coverage, and I feel like an idiot, standing here as the traffic whizzes by. But I must time this meeting right.

Three weeks have passed since Lacey turned me down. Or even spoke to me for that matter. Believe me, it hasn't been from my lack of trying. She completely ignores my texts. A guy's ego can only take so much, but I'm determined to make her see how serious I am about taking her on a date. I wanted to approach her sooner, but finding the time has been a bigger challenge than I anticipated. Between her schedule and mine, a gap finally opened.

Who knows? The timing may be better anyway. Hopefully, she'll be worn down after her workout and not so feisty.

I've put a lot of thought into our first date. I want a quaint, romantic atmosphere so we can talk and get to know each other. Sounds a little hokey when I think it in my head, but I want to impress her without appearing like I'm trying too hard. And I've visualized the perfect place.

I just need her compliance.

Lacey comes walking out with her traitorous friend Jocelyn. I love Jocelyn. She tells me everything I need to know about Lacey's schedule or any other pertinent questions I have. I should find some way to thank her.

My focus shifts to Lacey and her carefree smile that showcases those asymmetrical, sinful lips. She's fucking perfect. Well, except for her choice in baseball teams. That Mets baseball cap she's sporting has to go. I'm hoping to be signed by the Phillies this upcoming draft, and for some stupid reason, I want her to support that team. *My* team. Damn if she doesn't look cute, though. I pop a stick of gum into my mouth and wait for my cue.

Lacey says goodbye to her friend, and my entire body stiffens at the delicious sight in front of me. She goes from cute to sexy-hot in zero to sixty. Her tight yoga pants hug her round ass cheeks, and I swallow down a groan. Jesus, I can't wait to cup her ass while she grinds against each deep thrust I'm willing to give. I need to halt those thoughts. It's going to be awhile before we get to that stage —Lacey's certainly not a cleat chaser—but I'm willing to wait. Because I know we *will* get to that point.

When Jocelyn steps away, Lacey faces forward, and I find myself drifting naturally toward her. So much for the casual approach I'd worked in my head.

Lacey rears her head back as if I startled her. Auburn spirals fall to the side of her face, and my first reaction is to reach across and swipe the errant strands back in place. I refrain and clear my throat instead.

"Hey," I say.

She shoots her friend a glare before returning those agitation-filled eyes to me. Yeah, I definitely need to pick up something for Jocelyn.

"Heading to the gym?" The skepticism rings loud and clear as she takes in my jeans and T-shirt.

My attire alone screams no, but the lack of a gym bag leaves no doubt as to why I'm here. I should've put more thought into this encounter.

"No, I came to see you."

My confession draws another frown. *What the hell?* Most girls would turn to goo by that admission. But then again, Lacey Stark is not like most girls. Thank God.

"Why are you harassing me?" She swings her tote over her shoulder and resumes walking.

I sneak a peek at her toned legs and perfect ass before answering. "You won't return my text."

"I thought you'd get the hint."

"And I thought you'd realize I won't give up."

She's a step ahead of me, but I don't mind the view. Not at all.

"Sorry, Zach. I'm not into casual hookups."

"I'm aware, but I'm not looking for a casual hookup. I want to take you on a date. Go out with me."

"Are you even capable of dating? I've checked. Nobody has ever known you to take a girl out."

She's done some checking?

I'll admit her acidic tone stings, but she's interested in me whether she realizes it or not. A person doesn't inquire about someone if they're not interested. I step beside her, keeping in time with her pace.

"I'm capable of dating. I just never met anyone interesting enough to ask out," I admit and then lower my voice. "Until now."

She halts and turns to face me. Taking full advantage of the opportunity, I reach across and place the errant, curly strand beneath her baseball cap. Her slight shudder beneath my hand causes my gaze to dip to her plump, lower lip. My mouth moistens, and I want nothing more than to have those lips on mine. I'm fully aware of my heart beating erratically in my chest as I pull my hand away, but I don't understand the reason. I force my eyes to look back up and stare into those emerald greens that have reduced me down to a candy-ass stalker wannabe.

"I honestly want to take you on a real date. *Please*, give me a chance," I murmur.

"Hey, Zach, the team's looking great this year," a guy says, stopping beside Lacey and me. I'm not sure who he is because my focus never strays from Lacey.

"Thanks, bro, I like our chances." *And take the hint and go away.* I don't mean to be rude, but I'm not being interrupted. She's a breath away from giving me what I want.

"Uh, well … good luck this year," he says, stumbling over his words. Understanding must dawn on him because he trips over his feet, trying to get away.

I cock an eyebrow, still waiting for an answer.

"Why are you so interested? I mean, why me?"

She's trying to be strong, but her voice wavers. I'm wearing her down. The trace of defeat in her eyes fuels my desire.

"Because" is all I offer. I don't want to admit she drives me fucking wild. That she's all I think about when I'm not concentrating on baseball. Hell, I'm standing so close to her I want to reach out and take her lips in mine. End this back-and-forth dance she insists upon.

"Because why?" she murmurs.

Her eyes beg for answers, so I swallow my pride.

"You make me see past my primal desires. You make me want to get to know you. The real you." I don't move as I let her digest my words. The way her chest heaves up and down, there's no doubt in my mind she's feeling this—whatever this is—between us, too.

"Go out with me," I say, my voice demanding.

She inhales and releases a shaky breath. "Okay."

✖

THREE BOTTLES OF WINE LINE THE SHELLACKED WOODEN surface of the tasting bar. I know my choice, but I'm waiting for Lacey to decide her favorite. Even though my goal is to prove my worthiness to date, tonight's all about Lacey.

"Mmm, I think this one is the best." She replaces the glass on the slick surface and gapes up at me.

"Good choice." A smile stretches across my face. *Jesus, Zach. Get it together.* I'm grinning like a little schoolgirl crushing on the lead singer of a popular rock band, and all she did was pick the same variety of wine. What the hell is wrong with me? I shift my focus to the server.

"We'll take a bottle of the Happy Valley Red with two glasses." Lacey gives me a sideways glance but doesn't say anything. "And add a package of crackers with Colby and Pepper Jack cheese."

After I pay the server, Lacey picks up the plate of crackers and cheese while I grab the wine and glasses. We cut a path through the timber-framed tasting room and exit to the outside patio, the cool breeze greeting us as we search of a table. Soft jazz plays through the outdoor speakers, and I can't help but feel smug. Whether she's impressed or not, I sure am.

Finding a table isn't hard since we're the only ones brave enough to endure the elements. I just hope once the sun sets it doesn't get too cool. We settle into some patio chairs, her sitting beside me, to take full advantage of the sun's descent. This setting is exactly what I'd hoped to experience—quaintness along with a beautiful vineyard backdrop. What more could I want?

"Did you always want to pitch?" Lacey asks as I pour the wine.

She dives into the conversation effortlessly as if we've known each other our entire lives. The car ride here has been filled with meaningful conversation—the first time in forever with a female. Considering how reluctant she was to go out with me, our rapport has been easygoing, natural.

"I actually wanted to be a quarterback." I take a sip, wondering why I admitted that. I've never told anyone about my childhood dream. My family never even knew that bit of information.

"Yeah?"

"I'll have you know you're looking at Greenview's Pee Wee Quarterback Champ."

"What even is that?" She scrunches her nose and proceeds to place a slice of cheese on the cracker.

Her questionable tone makes me laugh. "A bogus title our coach made up. He printed certificates for every football position. Coach had us come in his office, which was the concession stand at the park, and warned against telling other teammates about our title because he was giving papers to everyone. He said mine was the only legit one. Of course, I told everyone. And even though everyone received the same speech, I knew my title was the only one to count."

Her shoulders shake as she about chokes on her cracker. "That's terrible," she manages to say in between coughs. She grabs her glass of wine, and I watch her plant those lips on the rim as she takes a sip.

"Nah. It built our confidence."

"Is he the one to blame for your cockiness?"

I pull my gaze from her lips, and the impish gleam to her stare makes me grin. "I'm cocky because I'm good at what I do." Her eyes darken, and I want to shout a big "hell, yeah." That's right, sweetheart. You keep imagining how good I am.

"So"—she clears her throat—"you traded one set of cleats for another?"

Damn, this girl gets it.

"Yep, eventually. When I first played baseball, I originally started in right field. Tommy Long was the star pitcher and also the coach's son. But I liked pitching. When I was home with Dad, I'd practice different pitches: fastballs, change-ups. You know, the easier ones you start out with. But no matter how good I was or how often my dad argued with the coach, there wasn't a chance in hell of me starting. That ass insisted my arm best served the team in right field. Looking back, I think he saw me as a threat." I shake my head and place my hand on her back, right above her jacket. Running my thumb across her smooth skin on the base of her neck ever so slowly, I add, "But poor ole Tommy..."

"What happened to poor Tommy?" she whispers, gazing deep into my eyes.

"Freaky accident between a bike and a speed bump. Needless to say, the speed bump won with him flipping over the handlebars. He ended up with a compound fracture officially ending his little league pitching career. His dad had no choice but to start me. Once I started, I never looked back."

Her body quivers as her lips part. It takes all the control I have not to devour that plump, lower lip. Fuck, I need to keep the conversation going. Otherwise, I'm going to cave. I force myself to look away and pour another glass of wine with my free hand. My other hand stays planted on her back. Maybe I'm skating with danger, but I love touching this girl.

"What made you choose sports media relations?" I ask.

"My love for baseball. You can say it's part of my blood, but since I'm a girl, I can't very well play professional ball." She reaches across to pick her glass up and takes a sip. "My grandfather had a promising baseball career. Unfortunately, he was injured and forced to hang up his glove. Mom may have been an only child, but she had five children."

She cocks her head and lowers her voice. "All girls."

"Wow, that's a lot of estrogen."

"Shut up!"

I laugh when she jabs my leg. She doesn't pack much of a punch, but her hand remains on my thigh causing tingles to shoot straight to my cock.

"It was ... challenging. Anyway, Grandpa may not have been in full form, but he still loved the game. So, he did the next best thing. He chose the girl most interested in baseball and practiced with her. I happen to be the lucky one." Her genuine smile throws me for a moment. It takes a second to regain my senses.

"What position did he play?"

"Pitcher."

Well, fuck me. I don't dare ask about the type of injury. At this point, I don't want to know, not with this lingering shoulder pain. My mind needs to be on track, and I won't succumb to suspicion and doubt.

"Did you come from a large family?" she asks as if sensing my need for a subject change.

"No. I have an older brother." I stop there not really wanting to delve much further. Her question is easy enough but certainly not the direction I want this evening to go.

"So, no estrogen besides your mom in the house?" Lacey raises an eyebrow as if daring me to speak against the female population.

A strenuous laugh escapes, but I can feel my expression slacken. I should've known she would inquire further. Lacey's too intuitive. But my sister isn't a subject I ever talk about.

"No, not anymore. I had a sister, Zoe. She was a year younger."

"Had?" she asks softly.

"Yeah." I puff out a breath. Thinking about Zoe is still hard even after all this time. "When I was ten, we were coming home from a family reunion and got into a car accident. She...she didn't make it."

"I'm sorry. I didn't know." Her fingers squeeze my thigh ever so slightly. The reassuring touch temporarily distracts me and calms the threatening anxiety swelling inside.

"It was a long time ago." I don't divulge anymore information. She doesn't need to know how much alcohol my dad consumed that day nor the fact the entire family had stopped functioning after that accident. Despite the drinking, up until that point, Dad was great. Afterward, it was as if he morphed into an entirely different person. No more backyard ball practices. No more attending games. No more anything. I push the ill feelings toward my father aside and concentrate on the girl beside me.

"Oh, look." She points to the last light of the sun. "This is the most beautiful time of the day."

I wouldn't know. I'm too busy looking at the other natural wonder. Lacey.

She leans in next to me, and I wrap my arm around her tighter as strips of burnt oranges and yellows dip behind the vineyard.

"Cold?"

"I'm okay."

Her shivers state otherwise, but as if on cue, a staff member comes out and lights a patio heater stationed in the far corner. Since we're the only ones here, I'm not surprised when he wheels the contraption behind us. Instant warmth spreads against our backs, along with relief. I'm not ready to leave the seclusion of Lacey's company.

"It's been a perfect spring so far," the elderly gentleman says.

"Yes, it has." *And it keeps getting better.*

"You kids attend Penn State?"

"We sure do. Graduate this year, in fact."

"1954 alumni myself. Best of luck to you. Enjoy."

We're back to ourselves, and our evening is enjoyable right until the time the other staff members join us and places the empty chairs against the wall. I glance at my phone, surprised by the hour. Eight fifty-five p.m. Five minutes before the winery closes. It's way too early to end the evening, but going to a crowded bar doesn't sound the least bit appealing. I'm rather enjoying our seclusion and don't want to share her. No doubt, there will be a second date, but she's mine tonight. And I'd like to keep it that way.

We drive back through the residential area that led to the winery, and the metallic gleam from the slides catch my eye. A plan quickly formulates as I point to the park.

"You up for the swings?"

A smile tugs at her lips. "You may have been pee wee quarter-back champ, but I was the queen of the swings."

"Oh, yeah?"

"Yeah. Nobody could arc as high as me."

"Did the peasant boys grovel at your feet?" I'm half-teasing, but the thought of guys vying for her attention tightens my stomach.

The sarcastic laugh that resonates from her relaxes the sudden urge to claim her.

"Hardly, that would be my sister Nicole. She's the prissy one. I was too much of a tomboy."

"I bet you looked cute in overalls." I pull into a parking spot and kill the engine. "I already know you're sexy as fuck in a baseball cap."

The iridescent lighting from the street lamp cast enough glow to see the blush sweep across her cheeks. My gaze drops to her mouth for, like, the hundredth time this evening. Jesus, I want to know what she tastes like.

"Race you," she says, then turns, and jumps out of the car.

Oh, game on.

I hop out and chase after her. Lacey has a slight lead, but the advantage belongs to me. I'm in the best shape of my life. There's no chance in hell she'll outrun me. Mere seconds later, I close the gap between us.

She yelps as I grab her waist and pull her against my chest. My intentions were to spin her around and place her behind me so I'd be in the lead, but as soon as my fingers wrap around her hips and her bottom presses against me, I can't stop my motions. I pivot her body to face me instead and suck in a breath. Her flushed face mixed with her grinning and panting between laughs entrances me. She's fucking beautiful.

Her laughter trails off as she takes in my serious expression. The next moments occur so fast I'm not sure what happens. I don't know if it's her hands that begin massaging my pecs, my fingers digging deeper into the softness of her hips, or the way her tongue darts out to lick that luscious lip I've been craving, but whatever the reasons, our mouths collide in a fiery passion. I can't get enough of this girl. Her lips part, and I thrust my tongue forward, staking a claim on her lips, teeth, and mouth. That sweet mouth that tastes of my new favorite wine.

Lacey's hands trail to my head and grab a fistful of hair as my fingers work their way up under her jacket, landing just below the curvature of her breast. *Jesus, why does this feel so right?* I suck in her lower lip and bite down with the slightest pressure as my thumb skates across her pebbled nipple. The semi I've been sporting for most of the evening hardens to full mast when the sexiest moan vibrates against my mouth. I inch my free hand lower to her round ass and pull her even closer. I want her to feel how hard she makes me.

Lacey breaks our kiss, angling her head just enough to expose the soft, pale flesh of her neck. I may whimper as I plant my lips in the crook of her neck, nipping and sucking a trail to her collarbone while squeezing and tugging her nipple through the multiple layers of clothing. She grinds her pelvis against mine, making my dick strain further against my jeans, so tightly it's almost painful. Shit, I've never wanted anyone so badly in my life. I need to stop before we end up having sex. I like this girl and really want to treat her right. Fucking her in public on the first date doesn't constitute as treating her right.

I force myself to stop and back away. Pure lust radiates from our bodies, fueling the battle between my desire and conscience. The rise and fall of her chest along with her sexy-as-hell wanton expression wreaks havoc with my self-control. But I abstain. For once, I'm playing by the book because this time I actually care.

"Sorry, I got carried away," she says between pants, still eying me with a heated expression.

"I think we both got carried away." The realization of what we shared doesn't go unnoticed. That kiss was fucking hot. The hottest I've ever had. I continue to hold her stare as I add, "We're so doing that again. And soon."

CHAPTER SEVEN

LACEY

CURRENT DAY

THE NEXT BATTER STRUTS TO THE PLATE, THE SAN DIEGO skyline providing a gorgeous backdrop. Petco Park is a dream. I'll have to thank my boss when I'm through being mad at him.

The giant *FriarVision* LED video board shows the next batter's face. Jaxon "Jax" Carrigan, another Penn State alumni. I shake my head. It's like a Penn State blast-from-the-past reunion.

Despite not wanting to rejuvenate the "good old days" and the fact I'm surrounded by Padre fans, a sense of pride swells inside me. I always liked Jax. He matched Zach's cockiness, but he was nice once you peeled back his outer layer. A sports communication major like myself, I got to know him through our shared classes. I wasn't surprised when the Phillies locked him into a five-year contract at the beginning of this season. The team's positioning themselves to be contenders for the World Series, and Jax is a great asset bringing a .354 batting average. Not to mention, he's Zach's best friend.

But Jax deserved the deal. Drafted straight to the minors his junior year, he didn't have an awesome contract in place like Zach.

Zach's agent, Darrel, made the Phillies pay to acquire him. That's not common. Most players make the minimum for five years before the teams "show them the money." And that's only if they make it once they're pro. Not everyone signed to the minors makes it past the original five years, whether they're called to the pros or not.

Jax steps to the plate and stares down the pitcher. My guess? He won't be seeing a first-pitch fastball, especially since he's known for going after the first pitch.

The Padre's pitcher glances at the runner on first and then positions into the windup. He stretches and throws—a hanging curve ball, even better.

Crack!

Ah. There's no better sound than the baseball connecting with the bat's sweet spot. I snap my head to the left field and freeze, afraid any slight movement, like breathing, would somehow jinx the outcome. *Fly, baby, fly.* The ball soars through the air. The outfielder shuffles backward until he's flush against the wall. I fist my hands beside my thighs as the lead runner rounds second base. With two outs in the top of the fifth, it's all or nothing.

The left fielder jumps and stretches his gloved arm just as the ball grazes the tip of the leather. The ball lands safely into the bleachers, and collective moans break around me as the Phillies take the lead four to two. *Way to go, Jax Carrigan.*

The next Phillies batter flies out to the right, ending the inning in anticlimactic fashion. But we have the lead as Zach comes to the mound. Pre-game chatter has Zach on a low pitch count. How many pitches he'll be allowed to throw shall prove interesting. Per the press releases, the MRI came back clear. I find that hard to believe. Something is going on inside him. Although, he's been throwing relatively well thus far and showing no signs of pain. I should give him the benefit of the doubt, but something feels off. Women's intuition? Sixth sense? Whatever preferred label is attached, the haunting sensation won't leave.

Zach takes the pitcher's mound. He inhales and slowly releases, then winds up, and throws. Fastball down the middle. The batter gets jammed and pops the ball to the second baseman. *First out.*

The next out proves just as easy, and I foolishly think he'll have a quick one, two, three. But that is not how the baseball gods work. Zach gets ahead quick enough, but the batter runs the count full. I've been studying Zach the whole game. He's been an iron horse pitch after pitch. Right up until now. Now, he's showing subtle signs of wear.

Zach shakes off a couple of signs from the catcher, AJ Gonzalez, and then nods. He positions himself, and his next move happens so slighty it's barely noticeable. I'm surprised I even picked up on it. That darn twitch. My heart sinks at the realization he's still having pain. He steps off the mound and grabs the rosin bag. He's stalling. Finally, he gets back in position. As soon as the ball crosses the plate, the batter fouls it off along with the next six pitches. Zach releases another pitch and the foul ball lands in the left section beside me. *Argh, so close.*

All the times I've been to baseball games, I've never caught a foul ball. Then again, I've never sat this close. I'm surprised the *New York Times* scored this seat. I'm sitting in section 103 near the Phillies dugout and their batter's circle. This spot had to set the company back a pretty penny, and I didn't know the *New York Times* had a budget to send me here for this story. In fact, I'm surprised by the whole trip. *How can they justify spending this kind of money?*

Zach throws the next pitch, and the ball loops into the middle. Cheers erupt around me, but I internally groan. The next batter is a lefty with a batting average of .374. He's been hot today, already hitting a homerun and a double. The umpire calls time, and Coach McFay joins Zach on the mound motioning to his left arm. Interesting. Replacing a left hander for a left hander. Zach must be on a strict pitch count.

The scowl on Zach's face doesn't hide his frustration. As he steps off the mound, he shakes his head and swears. I know he wants to finish this inning. He can't get the win if he's taken out this soon. But the last batter ran up the count, and this move confirms the fact they're keeping their eye on him. Relief from knowing he's being taken care of tries overtaking my emotions, only to be sucker-punched down by the looming problem.

The anger displayed on Zach's face along with his sluggish pace back to the dugout makes me feel sorry for him. For a split second, I worry he'll glance over and notice me in the crowd. I've been relatively safe thus far since he's been focused on the game.

Zach gets within ten feet of me, and some jackass seated two seats to my right yells, "Go home, Pritchett."

Zach automatically jerks his head toward the sound, but his gaze lands and locks with mine. His eyes widen in surprise before he smiles. *That damn smile.* My insides tighten as I raise my right hand into a tiny wave. He nods in acknowledgment and exits to the dugout. Good Lord, what have I done?

As I leave the post-game press conference, I'm a little confused and conflicted. Zach's absence summons up a defeatist feeling, but I ought to be happy. Not being able to see him is exactly what I want. He needs to stay away from me as much as I should stay away from him. But if that's the case—which it totally is—then why do I feel disappointed? There's enough material to make a story. And I know the direction in which I'm taking it, but his pain is *not* the main focus. It doesn't matter if that's what my boss is paying me to do. I won't jeopardize Zach's career.

"Miss Stark."

I turn to a young gentleman walking toward me. He's dressed in a uniform, but he can't be older than fifteen. Perhaps, he's the ball boy.

"Ma'am, I need you to follow me."

"And why would I follow you?" I ask, a little flabbergasted.

"Um, a friend wants to ask you a few questions."

I quirk an eyebrow. "And who may this friend be?"

"Uh..." The kid bites his lip and glances behind him. "I can't say. I'm just supposed to summon you. If you could follow me, please?"

I suppress a smile. "Fine. Let's go see who your mystery friend is." Walking through the corridor, my stomach tightens. There's only one person here who would want to speak to me. Nobody in San Diego knows who I am.

The kid pushes the metal door forward and holds it open for me. As soon as I step inside, the identity of mystery man is resolved as Zach emerges from the dark corner. The swish of the door swinging shut resounds through the open space like a heckler at a golf tournament, and I'm very aware we're together in a dark, vacant room.

"I wasn't sure you'd come."

He's far enough away that I can keep my wits about me, but my nerves play havoc with my body. The last thing I need is to be alone with Zach Pritchett.

"I shouldn't have." My voice is low but strangulated. All I have to do is turn around and walk back out the way I came in, but my feet stay grounded.

"Yes, you should have."

An awkward beat of silence descends upon us, and it's partially my fault. I'm sure Zach's picking up my indecisiveness to stay or flee. He was always attuned to my needs and desires.

"Where are you staying?" he asks.

"Does it matter?"

"It matters to me." He takes a step closer but maintains a modest distance. "I really do want to talk to you, Lacey. To catch up. Just meet me."

I don't know if it's his constant pursuit, the knowledge of knowing he won't stop, or my own weakness when it comes to this man, but the next words fly out of my mouth before I can rein them in.

"I'm staying at the Manchester Grand Hyatt, not far from here."

A slow smile develops across that strong, chiseled jaw. "That's the same hotel we're staying at."

Of course, it is.

"Meet me in the bar on the top floor in about two hours," he demands.

It doesn't take long to realize this Zach is the same Zach from college—always getting his way. I relent to his request and nod.

"I'll be there." Before I cave to anything else, I turn to leave.

As my hand turns the doorknob, Zach hollers out, "Don't leave me waiting this time."

I suppress my smile. The thrill of knowing he waited on me shouldn't course through me, but it does. I glance over my shoulder. "I'll be there."

THE BARROOM CHATTER REDUCES TO MURMURS WHEN I SPOT Zach seated in the far corner. I pause for a moment to take in the sight. The intimate table nestled against the floor-to-ceiling windows provides a spectacular view of the Bay Area. That scene mixed with the room's warm lighting and atmosphere makes a perfect romantic setting. Did he realize this when he asked me to meet him here? My twenty-two-year-old self would've been quite impressed, but now? Not so much.

Zach hasn't spotted me yet. He's chatting with a gentleman who's standing beside Zach's chair.

I toss my shoulders back and pad across the carpeted floor one step at a time. *I can do this.* I'm halfway to the table when Zach's eyes zero in on me. The casual grin breaking across his face causes my stomach to flip. *What the hell?* I'm a grown woman for Chrissakes. I'm too old and bitter to respond this way.

Meeting him was such a bad idea, but I can't force myself to retreat. Instead, my legs keep marching forward as Zach gives a dismissive wave to his colleague. A knowing smirk crosses the gentleman's face as he turns to see who's stealing Zach's attention.

I tamp down the instant rage that swirls through my veins and press onward. No matter what this bozo thinks, there won't be any sexual liaison between Zach and me. Just a meeting that I may as well get over with, now. Zach won't stop until he gets his way. And tonight, yeah, this is just a one-time meeting. After tonight, Zach will be out of my life. Permanently.

I swallow back the remorse that statement causes and half-smile at Zach's greeting. He stands as I sit across from him.

"I'll get you something to drink. What would you like?"

"It doesn't matter. Red wine is fine."

Zach nods, and as much as I don't want to, I can't help but watch his retreating backside. His dress slacks enhance the round curves of his butt, and for a moment, I wonder if he has them tailor made. He looks that good.

Apparently, I'm not the only one to notice. Some tall, slender blonde makes her way to the bar and invades his personal space. As she leans her half-exposed chest into his side, my throat tightens. There's absolutely no reason to be upset. I have no hold over him. What or *who* he does is none of my business. Face it. There's never a shortage of women for the baseball players to choose from—even in this classy setting—and I know Zach has had his share.

It's not as if I've Googled him or anything. Well, that's not true. I may have peeked at a website or two, but I was just keeping up with his impressive stats.

It's not my fault those searches led to sorting through countless images of the man himself. They were mainly from the baseball games and charity balls. I loved the ones of him concentrating on the mound. His strong jaw set in determination. But the ones with him looking rather buff in a black tuxedo weren't too shabby either. They were, however, the most disturbing. In those pictures, Zach was never alone. The same type of girl—tall, lanky, and blonde—always accompanied him. But the pictures never showed him with the same girl. Nor were there ever any redheads. Not that it matters. Those model-like women would be more fitting for him than my non-slender ass. As much as I try not to let his indiscretions bother me, I must admit seeing it firsthand is rather prickling.

I face forward as he politely shakes his head, seemingly turning the woman down, and shifts away from her.

Take that, Blondie. Score one for the redheaded team. God, did I really just think that? Me caring is the last thing I need him to see.

He returns to the table and places the wine glass in front of me.

"Hopefully, the Cabernet Sauvignon will work."

"I'm sure it's not Happy Valley"—I raise an eyebrow—"but it'll be fine."

A warm smile crosses his lips as he takes his seat. "Lacey, you look good. You're more beautiful now than ever."

I've had my share of pickup lines in the past. Granted, not many but enough to know when someone is bullshitting. And Zach is not bullshitting. The intensity he radiates informs me differently. A rush of chills shoots straight to my core at the recognition behind that intensity. His gaze drops to my cleavage that's blossomed along with my hips. It may have come with the extra ten pounds I've gained since he left me. I shift in my seat and push away the night that I tried seeing him again. It hurts too much.

"You're handsome as ever. But I suspect you know that."

His cocky ass smirk returns. "It's always good to have your approval."

I don't say anything and take a sip of wine. I need the whole wine barrel to get me through this conversation. Maybe a barrel with a straw? Or better yet, a funnel.

"So, what have you been doing for the last five years?" he asks.

"After my internship, I went to work at the *New York Times*. Larry James hired me as an assistant in his office. A sports journalist position finally became available, and he offered me the spot. Honestly, I think he's staging his exit."

"I knew that bastard always liked you. So, Larry's ready to retire?"

"I think so. Believe it or not."

Zach's eyes narrow as his lips purse. I shift in my seat under his scrutiny.

"I thought you wanted to work in sports media relations. Why the change five years ago?"

I swallow down the threatening bile that suddenly rises and plaster on a fake smile. I pick my glass up and take another sip before answering.

"After my internship ended, that job wasn't something I could pursue."

A flash of confusion crosses those beautiful blues, but fortunately, he lets it go. I breathe out in relief. A quick change in topics is due. Stat.

"Thanks for the bottle of wine you sent me the other day. That was considerate." *Way to go, dumbass. Steer him to the past.*

"That night was one of my favorite memories"—he pins me with a look—"but not my most favorite one."

I feel the blush spread across my cheeks. *Dang it. Why do those memories haunt me?* I know which particular moment he's referring to. I know this because it's my favorite one, too. No matter how much I want to hate it.

He places his hands on mine. "I've missed you."

"Please stop. I don't want to go down that road." I withdraw my hands and place them on my lap.

"Tell me you haven't missed me, and I'll let it drop."

I suck in a painful breath and gulp down the truth that's on the end of my tongue. Of course, I've missed him, but I can't let him know that. Crap, I'm not strong enough for this, but I must be. Breaking eye contact, I place my hands back on the table and work the napkin under my glass. "It's more than over between us, Zach. It has been ever since you walked away from me."

"I only walked away because I didn't know any better. Fuck, I was so focused on making the pros, that's all I could think about. I thought letting you go was the right thing to do. The fair thing to do." He leans forward, but I continue staring at my drink. "Look at me."

A tightness squeezes my chest, but I shake my head no. His hand reaches under the table and lands on my knee.

"Look at me," he says gently. My body tenses from his touch, from his intense stare. "I did love you. Don't ever question that."

Oh, but I do. Every day since finding out our relationship was a stepping stone. Maybe his confession of love is supposed to help heal the gash that was left, but hearing him say "loved" in past tense opens the wound further. My stupid heart. *Be strong, woman!*

"I *loved* you too, Zach. That's why I let you leave without any protest." A pained expression crosses his eyes, but he doesn't say anything. Maybe witnessing his remorse is all the validation I need. *Maybe.*

Zach squeezes my knee, his thumb tracing small circles on the inner portion. It feels so good and has been so long since I had a man's touch a part of me wants to take him back to my hotel room. Want darkens his eyes as if he can sense the carnal changes in my body.

My gaze sweeps to Blondie who wasted no time hitting on another guy. Nameless blondes parade through my mind, snapping me out of this lust-induced coma and bringing me back to reality. Crap, it's not like I'm totally honest about our breakup, and he's better positioned today for the wild streak inbred in him.

"Enough of that. What's going on with you? You're still favoring your shoulder," I ask.

"Lacey, we need to talk—"

"No! Memory Lane is closed. Time to move on." I nod to his shoulder. "What's going on? Off the record."

He huffs and shakes his head. "I never could get away with anything around you, could I?"

But yet, you tried.

"You're evading the question."

Pulling his hand away, Zach leans back, and I hate how I miss his touch. He lifts his beer to his mouth and takes a swig before plopping it back on the table. With a slight shake of his head, he curses before picking at the label. I suppress a sigh. Zach doesn't need to tell me the truth about his shoulder. I already know.

"No, the pain isn't going away."

"You need to be honest with the coaching staff this time. If that means going on the disabled list, then go on the D. L."

"We have a good shot at making the playoffs this year. The team's talented, and the motivation is the highest I've ever seen." He looks up from his bottle and looks directly at me. "I don't want to miss being a part of it."

"Maybe it's tendinitis. Like before."

A non-humorous laugh rises from his lungs. "Perhaps. But this time it feels different."

"What are you going to do?"

"Nothing."

"Why am I not surprised?"

"You know me too well."

"Do I? The Zach I knew would be pissed at me for outing his pain in front of the world."

He presses his lips together and nods, concentration back on his bottle. "I wasn't too thrilled."

"Then why are you even talking to me?"

He leans forward and faces me straight on, those stormy blue eyes trapping me in my seat.

"It's been five years since seeing the only girl I've ever loved. I wasn't going to let one tiny deceit get in the way of a reunion."

I gulp. His confession is all-consuming, playing havoc with my self-control. But he didn't love me. How could he? The first chance he had, he fucked some cleat chaser. I need to leave before I end up saying or *doing* something regretful.

"It's late. I really should be getting back to my room. I have an article to write and an early flight."

"It's a little weird, you writing about me."

I remain quiet, not enjoying the position I've been placed in.

"Put me in a good light." He winks.

"I'll do my best."

"Thanks for meeting me. It's been great catching up." He stands and extends his hand. "I'll walk you to your room."

"That's not necessary." I try waving him off but to no avail.

"Like you said, it's late. I insist."

His stern voice clamps down any attempt at a rebuttal. There's no sense in arguing with Zach Pritchett. Instead, I reach for his hand and ignore the traitorous sensations that race through my body.

With our fingers intertwined, Zach leads me toward the elevators. Quietness descends upon us as he pushes the down arrow. I don't know why I'm holding his hand. I need to let go, but I don't. His warmth feels too good.

I'm saved, at least temporarily, as the doors slide open and Zach releases his hold. But when we step inside, he places his touch to my lower back, and that location doesn't pan out any better for my nerves. I turn toward Zach's raised eyebrow.

"Fourteen," I say.

My heart thrashes inside my chest. I haven't been confined to tight quarters with Zach for years, but my body acts as if no time has passed. As if yearning for his touch is the most natural thing to do. Luckily, my mind knows better.

Zach waves his key card in front of the fob and presses the number. He steps back and stands next to me, his arm brushing against mine. I absolutely don't shiver. No way. That was a chill because I'm cold. Yeah, the air in this elevator is cold. That's why it's difficult to breathe. Also, the sideways glance from Zach has nothing to do with the heat rising on my cheeks. Sweet Jesus, it's suddenly warm in here. What the hell is wrong with the air quality controls?

I swallow hard and pace my breathing as the elevator descends. I'm not sure if the queasiness in my stomach is from the sudden movement or Zach's proximity.

I risk sneaking a peek at him. It was meant to be quick, but that sexy half-grin that always manages to mesmerize me is present. I freeze, tossed into another memory.

A wave of heat darkens Zach's eyes that stimulates another shiver and electrifies my every nerve ending. He closes his eyes and takes a deep breath as if to calm himself. Upon opening them, there's no denying the lust hidden in the deep blue hues. He opens his mouth, but no words form.

"What?" I encourage, my voice throaty.

"Do you remember our first elevator ride?"

It's that memory mixed with him being so close that has my girl parts screaming for an encore. Not so much for the actual ride that night but what had followed.

"Yeah, I remember that night well. All too well."

He leans down next to my ear, and a hint of spearmint fills the space.

"We will recreate that night. I promise."

I gulp.

I'm so screwed.

CHAPTER EIGHT

ZACH

FIVE YEARS AGO

THAT FRESH, EARTHY SCENT THAT OCCURS AFTER A SPRING RAIN permeates the air as Lacey and I walk back to my place. With our hands intertwined together, being with her feels like the post-rain —the most natural, relaxing thing in the world. Even though this is the first time she's coming to my apartment—the first time to be intimate—I've anticipated having sex with her for so long it just feels right.

This past month of dating Lacey has been incredible. She's totally perfect. She's not clingy or all-consuming, which works great since my schedule is tight. The last thing I want is a girl to distract me from baseball, but Lacey's different. She has her own career path, and she's driven. That girl has a work ethic that mirrors mine.

But what I like most? I can be myself around her, and she accepts who I am.

I always thought dating someone would be a burden. As if I'd have to morph into some type of patsy. I'll admit, I can be domineering at times, but Lacey lets me be myself in a way that doesn't undermine her.

It fucking kills me that our relationship is temporary, but we're enjoying the time we have left. I've been honest from the beginning. Not hiding the fact I'm devoting all efforts into baseball. I have to. I have too many people depending on me. My brother is self-sustaining, but my parents are a different story. After Zoe's death, they shut down. My dad turned to alcohol to cope, and my mom just exists. They need the financial support my career can bring.

As far as sex goes, I've been good. No matter how loudly my dick screams at me—clearly tired of my self-satisfying actions—I haven't touched her. Lacey's unlike the other girls. I want our sex to mean something, and part of me doesn't want her to think I'm using her. Does that make sense? Perhaps I am turning into a putz.

Although I've raised the bar with Lacey, that doesn't mean I haven't thought about the ways I want to take her. To make her come so hard she'll be in a sex-induced coma. We've come close to sealing the deal a few times, but the timing hasn't been right. Tonight's different, though. Tonight, she's all mine. And I'm not stopping until I hear my name screamed from the top of her lungs.

What makes tonight great is the fact we have the whole apartment to ourselves. The team has a rare Sunday off, so the twins headed home for some family event. And even though Jax is warming up to the idea of Lacey and I dating, he still bailed for the evening. He plans on staying away until morning. I'm sure he'll have no problem finding a hot little number who'll be more than accommodating for the night.

"Watch the puddle." I yank her arm to pull her toward me. A pain spans across my back down to my elbow, and I can't stop my wince.

"How's your shoulder doing?" Lacey asks.

Shit. The girl has hawk-like senses, seeing and hearing everything.

"It's still tender," I admit. We resume walking along the sidewalk. "The final diagnosis is rotator cuff tendinitis."

Lacey nods but stays quiet for a moment. Having a grandpa sidelined with a rotator cuff tear, she's all too aware of the implications. She opened up about her grandpa one evening last week and explained why he never returned to baseball. Although I wanted to hear her story, the selfish side of me didn't. She did, however, convince me to tell my coaches and get my shoulder checked. Thank goodness, it's nothing serious. Which brings up another point, her outstanding knowledge of baseball is yet another thing we have in common. Like I said, she's perfect.

"I know rest isn't an option for you, but, Zach"—she tugs my arm to make me halt and stares up at me—"please promise to stop and get some rest if the pain gets worse."

"I will." Her unspoken concern makes my throat thicken. A desire to wrap myself around her and kiss away the stress lines consumes me. It takes all my strength not to maul her on the sidewalk. I pull myself together and resume walking. "They're giving me a cortisone shot on Monday. I'll be fine. After the season ends, I'll be able to rest then."

She laughs. "Yeah, okay."

"What? I will." I squeeze her hand. "I promise."

"You'll have about a week before the draft. Then if the Phillies—"

"When not if." I *will* get that signed contract with them.

"*When* the Phillies sign you, you'll start pushing yourself harder." She peers at me from the corner of her eye. "I know you, Zach."

The corner of my mouth twitches. It's nice having someone care about me. Not about my ability to throw a ninety-five mile per hour cut fastball or my wicked curve ball. Not about the projected money I'll be earning. But to only care for *me*. It's nice. Hopefully, in less than an hour, I'll be showing how much I care for her.

"I'll be sure to rest it," I reassure her and then point to the apartment complex off to the right. "My castle."

"Nice." She nods in approval.

We step inside the building's entrance and walk straight ahead to the elevator. Lacey sucks on her bottom lip as I hit the upward button, and I feel the need to clarify my intentions. Usually, the girls I hook up with know the score, but tonight's certainly no one-night stand. Tonight's just the beginning, or for a few months, anyway.

"Before we head upstairs, I want to make sure you know that you *are* mine. At least until the end of school. I can't promise any longer than that." But I certainly don't have any intentions of letting her go until then.

Her pupils dilate, and her eyes become heavy-lidded. "I'm banking on it," she whispers.

A pang of yearning jolts through my entire body. Why the fuck her ex-boyfriend dumped her is beyond me.

The elevator doors slide open, and I lower my hand to the small of her back, allowing her to enter first. I'm extremely horny and wanting Lacey is something I've fantasized about since seeing her on the baseball field. So, the tightening in my pants and the wild thrashing of my heart isn't surprising. It's this overall anxiousness of getting what I want that surprises me. I've never wanted any girl so badly in my life as I want her. Need her. I think a part of me would die if she didn't want this. But I would wait. She's definitely worth the wait.

I drop my arm as we face forward, and then I reach to hit the seventh-floor button. I suck in a slow, calming breath as the lobby disappears and the elevator jolts upward.

Lacey's breathing pattern changes to short pants, and I steal another glance. She looks at me through the corner of her eye, and the air suddenly becomes thicker. Charged. I can't breathe as warmth overtakes my body. Her flushed face tells me she's feeling the same way. *Fuck!* I can't take it any longer. I fucking crave her touch.

Her chin lifts, exposing her neck, and all my self-control breaks. I pull her body next to mine and back her against the wall. My mouth zeroes in on her soft, flushed skin she so graciously offers, and I savor every tiny moan coming from her mouth. I grind my hips into her, my erection pressing against her abdomen. I slip my hand beneath her jacket, spreading it wide open as she thrusts her chest out. An invitation? *Hell yeah!*

Cupping her breast, I work my mouth along the crook of her neck up to her jawline. The elevator halts and the doors open. I lift off her and whisper next to her ear, "I can't wait to bury my cock deep inside you."

Her sharp intake of air and slight shudder brings a satisfying grin upon my face, but I swear there's a hint of a smile upon her lips as well. Mmm, I think my girl likes the dirty talk.

I grab hold of her hand and practically drag her to my apartment.

"The twins are gone, and Jax won't be back until the morning. I warned him that you'll be here."

"Anticipating me staying?"

"Baby, when I get through with you, you'll be too tired to leave."

She laughs. "Cocky much?"

There's a slight tease to her tone, but I don't miss the hint of curiosity. Her desire to find out makes me grin as we stop in front of my door. I lean down and barely graze her lips before responding, "Confident. There's a difference."

Her lips part as she draws a shaky breath. I can't unlock the latch quick enough. As soon as the door frees, I turn, and our mouths collide. We stumble into the apartment, peeling off our jackets the rest of the way as I stake claim to her luscious lips.

"Don't mind the mess. My roommates are slobs."

"I don't care," she manages to say between each peck.

Her fingers frantically unbutton my shirt while I grab the hem of her lightweight, V-neck sweater and tug it over her head. As soon as she's freed, she pushes my shirt open, and I quickly shrug it off. My mouth zeroes in on the exposed part of her breast. Damn, her skin is like silk. Rich and smooth. I reach behind and unhook her bra as her fingers work the zipper of my jeans loose. We keep inching our way to the bedroom, leaving a trail of clothes behind. By the time we're in my room, we're down to our underwear and still lip-locked together. We fall into bed, and I lean back on my knees to look at her. Her auburn curls splayed across my pillow look better than what any fantasy I've conjured. Those perfect tits, sporting pebbled nipples that beg for my mouth, don't hurt either. My gaze travels to her black, lacy thong that's even sexier against her creamy-colored skin. Jesus, my dick screams for a release. I'm trying not to salivate.

"What's wrong?"

"Nothing." The confusion in her tone brings forth my confession. "I'm just savoring this moment because the mental picture of you on my bed didn't compare to your real beauty."

Lust darkens her eyes. "Yeah?" she pants, and her legs slightly spread apart.

"Yeah." I crawl forward, continuing to hold her gaze. "There's one slight difference, though."

"What's that?" she whispers as she watches my predatory move toward her.

"You didn't have this on." I grab hold of the side strings of her panties and yank them off and then remove my boxers. "I'm going to slowly build up to a point where you'll be begging for a release. Then, I'm going to stop and fuck you hard and fast. Your body's mine for the night, Lacey. But you will enjoy it."

Her mouth drops in shock, but I connect mine with that wet pussy I've been craving for weeks. An "oh" escapes Lacey's mouth as her fingers fly to my head. I push one finger inside her while my tongue traces to her clit. "Mmm, baby. You're so hot and ready for me."

A pleasurable sound escapes her mouth, and I keep pumping my finger back and forth in a slow, rhythmical motion. I want to take my time with her. Tonight, I want to pretend we have all the time in the world with each other. Not the expiration date destiny has stamped on our relationship because of our career choices.

My tongue caresses the soft folds around her clit as my free hand snakes its way up to her exposed breast. As her body arches and bucks beneath me, her moans become more verbal. There's a point when I know a girl is close and Lacey's close. I suck hard on her clit and curl my finger upward inside, hitting her most treasured spot. Her body trembles almost violently, but I withdraw my tongue and fingers simultaneously and smirk at her much-disgruntled moan.

"Don't worry, babe. I'll take care of you." I playfully slap her butt cheek. "Turn on your side."

She looks at me questioningly but complies. I position her top leg forward a bit, opening that beautiful pussy to me. Running my hand along her curves, I then dip my finger inside and relish in the wetness.

"When I'm inside you, I want you to feel every inch of my cock." My voice comes out gruffer than I anticipate, but she has me so aroused. She's fucking perfect in my hands. Warm. Wet. Inviting.

Her whimper as I withdraw my finger sends a shiver through my body. Damn, I can't wait to be inside her.

"Patience, baby."

I slip the condom on and slide next to her, positioning the tip of my cock at her entrance. Without wasting time, I thrust forward until I'm buried to the hilt. The combination of surprise and pleasure that falls from her lips causes me to pause. Then I begin pumping back and forth, slow at first, enjoying every sensation her tight channel brings. My rate becomes faster, fueled by my racing heart, as her breathing becomes more vocal. I glide my fingers lightly across her skin until her breast fits inside the palm of my hand. I roll her hardened nipple between my fingers and tug with the slightest pressure. Her hands ball into a fist as she clutches on to the sheets with every deep plunge. She's so damn tight. As her walls milk me, it takes every self-control technique I have not to lose it.

"You like that, babe?"

"Yes ... God, yes."

"You're so tight. I love being buried deep inside you."

She shudders, and I swear her pussy clamps around my dick tighter. I'm afraid this pleasure isn't going to last much longer. I trace a path from her breast down to her clit and rub circles. Her body's primed, unable to take anymore stimulus. I plunge inward one last time, going as deep as possible. She unfolds in my arms, trembling as pleasurable waves convulse through her body. I crash on top of her, momentarily spent from what can be deemed as the best sex of my life. Holy shit, that felt great. The way she responded to every touch. Damn!

After a few moments, I collect myself and pull out of her. She rolls onto her back as I dispose of the condom. I lie back down and turn toward those beautiful green eyes. Lacey's right where I want her: ragged breaths, satiated expression.

"Where did you learn to do that?" she murmurs.

I laugh.

"I'm pleased with what my hands and tongue can do. These long fingers"—I wiggle my fingers back and forth—"weren't made for just throwing baseballs. They aim to please. But my dick? Now that, I'm quite proud of. And I do try to perfect *all* my skills."

"You have my vote for MVP."

In a swift movement, I slide on top of her, pushing myself up by my forearms. "We're just getting started, babe."

Her eyes grow wide, and I lean down, gently pressing my lips to hers. I run my fingers through her long wavy strands as I worship her mouth in a slow, tantalizing fashion. I'm taking my time this next round. Her body is a temple to be cherished. One to which I plan on paying homage to.

CHAPTER NINE

LACEY

CURRENT DAY

...Once again, Zach Pritchett showed dominance even with a limited pitch count. The win may not be his to claim, but Zach's perseverance proves nothing, not even shoulder tenderness, will slow him down. Zach will stop at nothing for the win.

"Great article." Jocelyn sets the paper copy on the kitchen table. She stands and meanders over to the coffeepot.

"Thanks. I think my boss was looking for a little more dirt." My jaw stiffens as I sit straighter. "I don't care. I didn't want to betray Zach."

Her lips twitch as she pours her coffee. She lifts the carafe up, and I glance down at my full cup and then shake my head. She doesn't say a word, but she may as well have. Her silence screams at me.

"Just say it. You know you want to."

"You know"—she sits back at the table—"as much as you claim to hate him, you really don't."

"Can we not talk about my feelings for Zach?"

Her mouth forms a tight smile, and she raises an eyebrow.

"*Please*," I beg.

"Fine. We can pretend you hate the prick. But you have to tell me if Zach's the same as he was in college."

"What? A cocky bastard? No, that hasn't changed." I take a sip.

"No! Is he still handsome as ever? You've seen Carl. He hasn't aged well."

I choke on my drink. Literally. Coffee burns the entire back of my throat, and I swear the sting extends into my lungs. Can a person drown from a sip of coffee? If the fire in my throat is any indication, the answer is yes.

"Your husband's good-looking." I try to scold after catching my breath. "He's only twenty-seven."

"He's developing a potbelly. I'm afraid he's going to turn out like his dad." She laughs. "Come on, spill. I'm dying. I've seen his pictures, and he looks fit."

"Of course, he's fit. He's a professional ballplayer with a daily workout routine." I roll my eyes.

"So, he still looks good?"

"Yeah," I snort. "He looks even better. More buff. How is that fair?"

"Dang it. I knew I should've gotten Carl that gym membership last Christmas."

I shake my head. Carl and Jocelyn dated almost the entire time in college. They met during the second semester freshman year—just like she and I did—and have been together ever since. She's madly in love with him, and it's apparent every time I come over to watch her kids during date night.

"But yet, you let him walk away last night. Just like that? Before even doing the nasty?"

I cringe and scan the area for little ears. Who uses the word nasty to describe sex anymore?

"Relax. The kids are still outside playing. You just answer my question."

"No. We didn't do the 'nasty,' as you so eloquently call it. I'd be lying if I said I didn't want to. You know I'm not going to get *that* started." I rest my head in the palm of my hand. It was hard saying goodbye to Zach and shutting my hotel door. "Honestly, being with him brings back all those feelings I've tried to forget. Zach always had a way of making me feel beautiful. Wanted. Well, until that dreaded last night. I can't go down that road. You, of all people, should know this."

Even though I can't see her, I feel her sympathetic look. Once again, her silence is stifling.

"What are you thinking?" I open my eyes and let my hand fall to the table.

"You know what I'm thinking."

"Yeah, well, I don't like what you're thinking. Plus, I disagree. Zach's at a crossroads between his shoulder pain and renegotiating his contract with the team. He needs to stay focused. They have a great shot at the playoffs this year, and I'm not adding to his stress. I can't. Just like five years ago, I wasn't going to be the one who ruined his chances then, and I'm not going to be the one who ruins it now."

"Okay, maybe the timing is bad, but what about at the end of the season? He'll have a break."

"Maybe."

"He deserves to know the truth behind your breakup."

"He broke up with me, remember? Our relationship was never supposed to be permanent. He made that clear from the beginning, and then that fucking awful night."

"You mean the one where you never confronted him?" Her accusatory tone pisses me off, but she's exactly right. He never knew I flew down to see him.

"That night destroyed me. I honestly thought he had used me the entire time we were together." My tone grows sadder as I continue, "Last night he confessed he had loved me."

"You two need to sit down and have a serious talk."

"I know." I slowly exhale as I shift my gaze to the window. "I'll see what happens with his shoulder this season. Then, I'll try."

"Fair enough. Does he have plans to contact you again?"

"No. We didn't exchange numbers, and I'm sure after talking to me, his itch is scratched...so to speak."

"You of all people know Zach doesn't stop until he gets his way."

"Yeah. I just need to make sure I'm not what he wants."

"No, you just need to make time to see him."

"Mommy. Mommy. Mommy." The kids come barreling inside the back door, cutting off my retort. I stand to leave.

"Thanks again for taking care of everything on short notice. I'm not sure what I'd do without you."

"No problem, but you know I'll collect."

As if on cue, little arms bombard me with hugs and knock me off balance. I laugh and weave my fingers through fine blonde ringlets. "Not a problem. You know I'm game anytime."

Carl steps into the kitchen and bends down to kiss Jocelyn.

"Hey, baby," Jocelyn says. "Good day at work?"

"Mm-hmm. Better now. But I have to go back tonight. Probably pull an all-nighter."

"But it's Friday."

"I know. I'll make it up to you."

They exchange a kiss, and the sincerity in each other's expression touches my heart. That's what I want—a partner to come home and appreciate me. Why is it so difficult to find?

"How was the trip?" Carl asks me as he removes his tie.

"It was nice. San Diego is amazing. I'm glad to be back, though."

"I'm kind of jealous your job makes you go to baseball games." He laughs and walks to the living room. He yells behind him, "I keep waiting for Dusty Baker's autograph."

"I'm working on it." I give Jocelyn an "oh shit" look. As she chuckles, I say, "I need to be getting home. Thanks again."

"Remember what I said." Jocelyn shoots me a look.

"Yeah, sure." There's not a chance in hell that I'll see Zach again. After our last visit, I'm sure he's feeling less guilty for leaving me and can return to his blonde model-type girlfriends. "I'll call you later."

✄

Y<small>ANKEE</small> S<small>TADIUM</small>. H<small>OME</small> <small>TO</small> <small>AN</small> <small>IMPRESSIVE</small> <small>TWENTY-SEVEN</small> World Series championship titles. This newer structure I'm standing in only has one World Series registered win, though. As I recollect today's events, I can't help but be impressed. One perk of my job compared to my original career choice is the different stadiums and teams I get to visit. Yes, it would've been nice focusing on one franchise, but let's face it, my heart will always belong to the Mets no matter where I'll end up. At least this way, I don't feel traitorous on either end.

The Phillies are back in town playing the Yankees for a few days during interleague play. These two teams don't meet every season, but this happens to be the year they do. *Just my luck.*

It's been three weeks since my last contact with Zach, and I'm not sure whether I'll see him this trip or not. I'd be lying if I said he hasn't crossed my mind during those three weeks. When I'm alone at night, my thoughts revert to our goodbye in San Diego. Standing at my hotel door, I'm not sure if he expected an invitation to come inside. He didn't act as if he did. In fact, he was a perfect gentleman. The only thing I can't deny is his longing. I almost caved from the heated look he had every time he looked at me. But he never acted on it, and neither did I.

Doesn't matter now. It's yet another chapter in the past, and since Zach isn't scheduled to pitch the entire three-game series, I doubt he'll seek me out. Regardless, my boss still insists that I cover the games.

Part of me wonders if I pissed him off somehow. But then again, he doesn't realize how Zach's constant presence tortures my feelings.

The Phillies crushed the Yankees today seven to two. Today's hero? Jax Carrigan. He went four for five, smacking in an impres-

69

sive five runs. He's definitely earning his spot on the team. This is one post-game press conference I'm anxiously awaiting.

"Great article on Zach a few weeks ago," Brayden says as he sits beside me. "I'm flabbergasted that the *Times* paid for a San Diego trip."

"Thanks, but I'm hoping not to travel too much."

"Embrace it. That's the beauty of this job." He winks just as Coach McFay waltzes in with Jax trailing close behind.

I shake off his comments and take notes as questions are directed to McFay and Jax. A guy next to Brayden speaks up, asking Jax a personal question. Jax shifts his eyes toward Brayden's voice but pauses when he takes in my presence. With a nod, he smiles in clear recognition.

"Sheesh," Brayden says, turning to look at me.

"What?"

"Are you friends with all the players?"

I double blink, not caring for his accusatory tone. In fact, I'm a little offended.

"Only the ones that I went to Penn State with." I hear shuffling about and know the post-conference has ended.

Brayden groans. "That totally came out wrong. I just meant—"

"Lacey," Jax interrupts, leaning down to pull me in for a hug. "It's great to see you. I'm so sorry I missed you in San Diego."

"It's great seeing you too, Jax." I back away and notice Brayden hovering by. "Oh, sorry. This is Brayden Hicks from CBS New York."

Brayden extends his hand to shake Jax's and then turns to me. "Lacey, I was hoping to get your number."

His statement throws me for a moment. Didn't we already do this back when Zach first approached me? "Uh, sure." I reach into my bag and pull out my card, remembering he only gave me his. As I hand it over, his warm smile puts me on edge.

"I'll call you sometime." Brayden turns to Jax and nods. "It's nice to meet you. You're a force on the field."

"Thanks, Brayden." With an arched eyebrow, Jax half-grins. "Looks as if Zach has some competition."

My heart skips a beat at the prospect of Zach wanting me. *Damn it.* That's not supposed to happen. I smack Jax's chest in protest. It's a familiar move. One I've done several times while dating Zach, except I don't remember Jax being a solid mass of muscle.

"I think we both know Zach and my ship sailed a long time ago."

"I'm not so sure. You're all he's talked about for the last three weeks. Lacey this. Lacey that."

"Oh, stop." I push his chest again, but he doesn't even budge. He just laughs instead.

"In all seriousness, Zach does want to see you. Can you come with me?"

"I don't think that's a good idea."

Jax purses his lips for a second.

"I can still kick his ass for hurting you." He quirks an eyebrow. "I may have to wait till postseason, though."

"There will be no kicking of any ass." My teasing tone trails off as my mood turns somber.

"Ya know, I told him he was an idiot for letting you go, but I honestly believe he thought he was doing the right thing. There isn't any doubt in my mind that he loved you."

I look up to the ceiling and swallow hard, blinking back the threatening tears. I don't understand what's wrong with me. I was over him. I mean, I am over him. *I think.*

"It's in the past and doesn't matter. What's seeing him now going to do but stir up hurt feelings?"

"Those feelings don't have to hurt," a deep voice says behind me.

My stomach plummets, and I turn toward the deep blue eyes currently haunting my thoughts.

"Zach," I whisper.

"I'm going to take off and leave you two to discuss things." Jax leans down for another hug and whispers against my ear, "Just hear him out."

I continue to stare at Zach, surprised that he came to find me.

"Can we go somewhere a little more private?" Zach extends his hand, and the gleam in his eye acts as if it's challenging me. At my hesitation, he drops his hand and sighs. "Please?"

Against my better judgment, I nod.

"Thank you," he says as he turns and steps forward.

I have no idea where we're going, but I follow him down the corridor anyway. About fifty feet into the hallway, we come across an unmarked door to the right. Zach wiggles the door handle and slips his head inside the room when the door freely opens.

"This works."

We step over the threshold, and as soon as I'm clear, he releases the handle. My eyes adjust to the scant amount of lighting peeking through the four tiny block windows on the far wall. The door slams shut, and I halt as Zach closes the gap between us.

"Go out with me tonight."

I take a step back, but Zach matches my footing until I'm backed against the cold metal door. He arches his arms over my head and leans forward, his chest pressing against mine. He studies me for a second and then repeats, "Go out with me tonight."

"I can't." My voice squeaks, and I hate how desperate I sound.

"Can't or won't."

"Both."

He brings his face within a breath's distance away, our lips barely brushing. My heart races and with each rise of my chest, our bodies connect, waking every nerve ending.

"Then I'll come over to your house. I know your address."

A slight gasp escapes my mouth, and I try to ignore the sudden rush of heat. There's no way Zach can come to my home. He just can't.

"I'll meet you. Anywhere," I say . God, I hope he doesn't question my sudden compliance.

"I'll pick you up around eight."

"No." I swallow, trying to keep from panicking. "I'll meet you at your hotel, and we'll go from there."

The corners of his mouth rise to a slow seductive smile. "Meet in the lobby at the Grand Hyatt at eight."

With the slightest inclination, I nod. He stares a moment longer, and I desperately want to escape. But there's a small part of me that wants to close the minute space between us. His gaze drops to my quivering lip, just as he did in the past when I knew he wanted to kiss me, but instead of leaning forward like I think he's going to do, he backs away.

"I need to get back before Coach has my ass in the ringer." He sidesteps around me and opens the door. "I'll see you tonight."

I don't respond as his long legs carry him down the hallway away from me. My heart paces back to normal, but wow, that was intense. This emptiness in my chest proves one thing. I wanted that kiss, more than anything. Jesus, how am I going to be strong enough to withstand tonight? Newsflash. I'm not.

CHAPTER TEN

LACEY

CURRENT DAY

THE CLICKING SOUND OF HEELS STRIKING THE TRAVERTINE marble floor halts when I catch sight of Zach seated by the expansive waterfall. He runs his hand along that strong jawline and studies the fountain as if he's deep in thought. The slim-fitted button-down shirt fits tightly across his broad shoulders, and I take a moment to collect myself again. I can't get caught between my past feelings and present hatred. And yes, despite what Jocelyn says, I hate him. I also hate that I have to keep reminding myself that. But as Zach turns and his eyes widen with heat, it's hard not to swoon. He looks so damn sexy.

In a swift move, Zach stands and then glides over to where I'm standing. His gaze roams along my body, and the sharp blue color from his shirt brightens his piercing eyes. Or maybe the shine generates from the obvious desire radiating from him. I swallow hard. *Oh hell, who am I kidding? I no longer hate him.*

"You look beautiful," Zach says with a slight strain in his voice. He takes a deep breath as if to calm himself.

I glance down at the jade-colored dress I borrowed from Jocelyn and self-consciously tug the hemline. A slow burn rises from my chest to my cheeks. I'm not used to wearing something so short, and I suddenly feel naked from all the flesh the off-the-shoulder sleeves exposes.

"Thanks. You don't look so bad yourself."

Zach grabs my hand, and we stroll to the main entrance and then wait for the driver. He turns to me with an impish glint in his eyes.

"When was the last time you went out and let loose?"

I study Zach, and for a fraction of the time, I wonder if he knows the entire truth. That's impossible. He wouldn't be standing beside me if he did.

"I live in New York City. I go out all the time." The lie slides easily off my tongue, but there's no way, I'm admitting the time-frame of my last date.

Zach's nostrils flare, and an all too familiar look crosses his eyes —the one that claims I'm his, at least for tonight.

A black Mercedes car pulls up and breaks the strange spell between us. I'm still a little dazed as we enter the back seat.

Now, Zach's tall, and his legs fill most of the space, so it's not surprising when his thighs brush against mine. Nor am I surprised when he interlaces our fingers. It's the warmth invading my system and shooting straight to my groin that catches me off guard. Holy crap, I can't be in confined quarters with this man.

I steal a glance at Zach. It's meant to be quick, but he's staring back with such intensity that I can't turn away. I need to, though. I shouldn't risk being sucked into the Zach Zone—the area where my heart reaches a point of no return.

He zeroes in on my mouth, and my lips part of their own accord. Zach inhales a sharp breath and tightens his hand around mine. With a slight shake of his head, he rapidly blinks a few times. At least, I'm not the only one affected by the other's presence.

Zach clears his throat and asks, "How's Grandpa Denny doing?"

What better way to douse a fire than to bring up my grandpa? I take a moment to collect my thoughts before speaking.

"Grandpa's good. He had a hip replacement a year ago, but he's pretty much recovered now."

Zach lowers his chin and stares at the floorboard. "I only met the guy once, but I sort of miss that old man."

I press my lips together, fighting a smile. During the graduation celebrations, Zach's presence was an instant hit, especially with Grandpa. I blame their baseball bond, but if I'm honest, Zach has a personality that draws people in. My family loved him, which made it that much harder when things ended.

"He's proud of you, ya know."

"I figured he'd hate me."

"No. It's not you he's upset with." I clamp my mouth shut, shocked by my confession. Confusion crosses Zach's face, but I'm not surprised. My statement was rather cryptic. I ignore his unspoken question and continue, "I know he secretly keeps up on your stats."

"Secretly?" Zach raises an eyebrow.

"Yeah. Well..." I stir in my seat, wondering why I opened my mouth. "No one's allowed to speak your name around me."

His back stiffens, and he withdraws his hand.

"God, Lacey, I can never apologize enough. Can you ever forgive me?"

Guilt consumes me. I should've kept my mouth shut. "I already have. It was a long time ago. We both did what we had to do."

"I wish I'd done things differently."

"Yeah, me too." *More than you can ever know.*

Zach sighs as the car creeps along in Friday night traffic.

"What about the rest of your family? Your mom, sisters."

I face forward and press my lips together. I wring my hands together like I do every time someone brings up my family. *Hurry up, driver, and get us there.*

"I haven't talked to them for a while, but I think they're doing okay."

"You guys were so close. What happened?" The sincerity in his voice tightens my chest. He returns his hand on top of mine.

"Um, we just had a falling out. Some things were said." I shrug. "It hasn't been the same since."

With a gentle squeeze, he lifts my hand to his mouth and sweeps a soft kiss across my knuckles. Lowering our hands to his lap, he says, "I'm sorry, babe."

"Me too." *In more ways than one.*

We arrive at a club, and Zach has no problem getting us past the bouncer. It's amazing what fame, or more like *money*, will do. A twinge of guilt passes through me as I eye the people standing in line, but with these four-inch heels Jocelyn insisted I wear, I have no desire to spend the evening waiting on the hard concrete. Plus, this is my first actual "club" experience. I do want to make the most out of it.

The electronic beats resonate through the air as we scope out a table. I scan the room, taking in the lights and decor. The orange and brown hues, along with the funky styles, has a seventies vibe to it. And people? There are tons of people crowding the sunken dance floor. How can they cram so many bodies together?

After a few glasses of wine, the crowd's no longer a concern. My upper muscles relax as the alcohol works through my bloodstream, but not even the strongest port could lessen the tension in my lower half. My legs burn with need from the magic of Zach's fingers softly caressing the inside of my thigh. It's like he cannot *not* touch me. His hands are constantly somewhere on my body. I want to push him away, but I want to maul him right here and now. This constant hot and cold feeling is driving me insane. I need to get up and move before I do something stupid.

"You ready to dance?" Zach asks.

"Born ready."

A low chuckle escapes his mouth as he follows me to the dance floor. If I thought dancing would chill my impure thoughts, I couldn't have been more wrong.

Time. Distance. Heartache.

It all seems irrelevant with our bodies molded together. Something that feels this right must be good. *How can it not?*

Those sensual hands I've been craving land on my hips, and he growls a deep guttural sound as he presses my backside against his lower half. We start to grind, practically dry-humping to the beat.

It doesn't take long to figure out Zach's own needs. Not when his impressive bulge rubs against my ass. I develop a quick love-hate relationship with the denim company, wishing the layers of clothing would disintegrate. I'm hyper-aware of the multiple orgasms his "bulge" can produce, and if I don't get some relief soon, I'll die from relentless want.

As if reading my mind, Zach spins me around and then crashes his lips upon mine. His hands move everywhere, exploring my sides, waist, hips, and ass. They finally rest upon my hips, and I practically unravel returning his kiss like the starved woman I am. The last thing I want is to embarrass myself on the dance floor, but it's been too long since I had a man's touch. *Zach's touch.* And my body is wired.

Zach pulls away. His gaze remains fixed on me, and our rapid chest movements sync together. I reach out to pull him back, but he grabs hold of my hands to stave me off. *What the heck?*

"Let's get out of here," Zach pants.

He motions his chin toward a dark hallway. I should protest, but I kind of fear the mutiny my overactive hormones would stage. I want this. *Need* this. I want to be reckless once with no responsibilities—only uninhibited adulterated sex.

I follow Zach down the hall to the flashing red and white exit sign. He pushes the door open, and a blast of cool, night air strikes our faces. I halt, and Zach turns toward me right as the door slams shut. We're alone in the narrow alleyway, trapped outside with the bustling sounds of the city in the distance as my heartbeat thrashes loudly in my ears.

"Fuck, I want you so badly," Zach says.

The next thing I know, my backside scrapes along the bricks. It's just this side of painful, but I don't care; the ache between my legs has worsened with need. I want Zach more tonight than I've ever wanted him.

Zach's hands cup the sides of my face as he leans forward. The moment his lips touch mine, my body lights with desire, and my mouth opens, allowing his tongue access. He deepens the kiss as he runs his hand down my neck to my shoulders and tugs the dress down exposing my breasts. His growl vibrates along my lips before he breaks away and takes my nipple into his mouth, scraping his teeth along my hardened flesh. His hand slips beneath my dress and snakes around to cup my ass. Tingles shoot straight to my core from the proximity of his fingers. He's so close to being able to pleasure me.

"Mmm, you dirty girl." His deep, velvety tone glides across my skin, and the quick smack to my ass cheek heightens every pleasurable erogenous zone. "You're not wearing any underwear. Did you do that for me?"

"No. Maybe." I can barely speak.

He palms my sex, his finger slipping between my folds, sliding into my channel.

"Fuck. You're so hot and ready for me." His mouth lands on my throat and sucks a path to my earlobe, his breath tickling my ear. "You feel so right. God, I've always loved your slick pussy."

Damn, that dirty mouth of his. He could always turn me on with his words alone. While moving his finger in and out, he sweeps his thumb in a circular motion over my clit. A hard shiver ripples through me. I'm so close to going over the edge.

"Oh no, not yet. You're not allowed to come until I'm buried deep inside."

He hikes one of my legs around his waist and then lifts me up. In a fluid movement, he pushes deep inside as both my legs wrap around his waist. *How'd I miss him undoing his pants?*

"Your shoulder," I pant. Stopping sounds awful, but I don't want to risk injuring his tender shoulder.

"I'm fine." And to drive his point home, he continues to thrust, hitting areas that no other man has ever come close to touching.

Pinned between the wall and Zach, I hang on to his broad shoulders. With each forward jab, the dress snags against the brick. I'll owe Jocelyn a new dress, but the expense is worth it. Zach's deep inside me, and I swear I feel each thrust from my shoulders to my toes.

Pressure keeps building, and I'm almost to the point where I can't take anymore. Zach rams hard and pauses. "I've missed you so much, Lacey," he cries out.

The lines cross between reality and fantasy. I no longer can tell the difference between my old feelings versus the new ones. I just know I missed him. Missed this. Missed us.

A sound crossed between a pleasurable cry and moan slips from my lips, and my body shatters into bits of ecstasy as Zach pumps his release into me. He stills with his dick buried deep inside.

"Not going to lie. I wanted to take you since that first press conference, but I pictured a more romantic setting," he says between pants. "But this was fucking perfect. You're fucking perfect."

My eyes grow wide as he pulls out of me. *Oh my God. What have I done?*

Zach must take in my expression. He sets me on the ground and helps steady my wobbly legs. I can't keep them from shaking.

"Hey, look at me."

I don't look. I can't. This enormous cock, covered with only our juices, takes top precedence. There's no condom. *Where the hell is the condom?* I bite my bottom lip. *Shit!*

"Hey, don't worry"—he tucks his dick back into his boxers and zips his pants close—"I'm totally clean. I never screwed anyone without protection. Well, except you."

That doesn't make me feel better. In fact, that confession makes me feel worse. I remain tight-lipped and stare at him.

"No one," he reinforces.

I shake my head.

"Come here." He tucks me in his arms and kisses the top of my forehead. "You're on the pill, though. Right?"

I'm silent for a beat. The conversation sounds way too familiar.

"It's okay," I manage to croak out.

CHAPTER ELEVEN

LACEY

CURRENT DAY

My fingers fumble with the shredded pieces of homemade bagel that Jocelyn slid across the kitchen table and insisted I eat. Food's the last thing I want at the moment. What I want is to hide, move, or get swallowed up into a hole and never resurface. Maybe I'm too dramatic, but what had I been thinking last night?

Vanilla wafts through the air, and my stomach welcomes the scent with a growl. Okay, maybe I'm a little hungry. I pick up a broken chunk and begin to nibble.

Jocelyn sets the pancake batter aside and, with her own bagel in tote, joins me and takes the seat across from me.

"I don't understand why you're so hard on yourself. You're twenty-seven years old. I think a walk of shame is way overdue."

"You're one to talk. You haven't had any. Besides, I'm not like most twenty-seven-year-olds."

"No, but I fail to see the problem."

"The problem? The problem is"—I glance at the living room, making sure there are no small ears overhearing, and then lower my voice—"I screwed him in a dingy alley like some cleat chaser we always made fun of."

She snorts. I'm explaining my life-crushing story to my best friend, and she snorts.

"Will you stop? I'm seriously freaking out here."

"Sorry." Jocelyn chuckles a few more times. "You're so far on the other side of the cleat chaser spectrum; it's hard not to laugh."

"I'm glad you find it humorous," I say in a flat tone.

"Okay, okay. I'll stop. But I still don't understand why you're so hard on yourself. There was never a shortage of passion between you two. Carl and I were afraid we'd get burnt from the sparks flying off you guys."

My mouth falls open. I'm not sure how to respond. Jocelyn does speak the truth. Or at least the partial truth. What Zach and I had in college was real. There's no mistaking that. And the sex ... phenomenal. But I always thought we controlled ourselves in public. I sigh and stick my bottom lip out.

"I ruined your dress."

She shrugs. "I'd say it's for a good cause."

This is what I love about Jocelyn. She's so carefree. That hasn't always been the case. Back in college, she was wound tight. Of course, having three kids may have taken away her "I give a fuck" passion.

"But what I really want to know." Her eyes widen with curiosity. "Was it good?"

"God, yes! I haven't come that hard for five years."

"Whoa. I didn't need to know that," a male voice rings out.

"Sorry, I can't believe you overheard that." Heat rises from my chest to my forehead.

Carl chuckles. "Glad ole Zach still has it in him. But you may need to change the subject. I don't want Jocelyn to start feeling slighted."

"Ah, baby. I'm completely satisfied."

Carl leans in and gives her a kiss, momentarily distracting her while he steals her bagel.

"Hey," Jocelyn protests as he slips away.

"I've got a few things to work on. I'll be in my office." He gets halfway across the living room before yelling, "Call me when the pancakes are ready."

Jocelyn laughs and shakes her head. "That idiot."

"You're so lucky."

"I know." She looks directly at me. "Your day is coming."

"Maybe someday. But until then, I blame my misery on you. If you hadn't given Zach my number back then, we wouldn't have gotten together."

"Please, he would've kept pursuing you. Zach's relentless when he sets his mind on something."

I let out a disheartening laugh. "That he is."

"I didn't give him your number for you to fall in love with him. I just wanted you to have a distraction from that asshole ex-boyfriend."

"Jason Kerr. I haven't thought of that ass in a long while. The night we broke up was the first time Zach talked to me." I laugh. "I wanted nothing to do with either one of them."

"Ha! That sure changed."

"I wasn't ever in love with Jason. I'm not sure why I was even with him."

"I wondered the same thing."

"Eh. Jason and my relationship was more out of convenience. That's why I never cared when it ended. But I never realized that until Zach wore me down and I agreed to go out with him." There's a vast difference between love and lust, and Zach brought that to light. "I have a confession about last night."

Jocelyn raises her eyebrows expectantly.

"I screwed him without a condom."

"You didn't." Her eyes widen as she gapes at me.

"Afraid so."

"How, why? You *know* better."

"Gah! I know. It just ... we got caught in the moment. Before I knew it, he was stick—"

"Okay! I get it." She starts to fan herself with her hand. "Holy cow. Did he say anything this time?"

"First he told me he was clean. He never screwed anyone without a condom before. Except me."

"What an asshole."

"Nah, he just doesn't have a way with words." Zach was an awesome boyfriend. He always put my needs first, up until he left for the majors. That meant more to me than a string of romantic words. "He then asked if I was on the pill."

"Jesus. You are, aren't you?"

"No."

"Oh, Lacey." Jocelyn covers her mouth with her hand, resting her elbow on the table.

"But I told him yes." My voice squeaks the word. I'm still shocked that I led him to believe he's off the hook.

"What?" Her arm drops to the table as disbelief clouds her expression.

"I know. Save me the lecture."

"You're a big girl. No lecture from me. I'm just ... wow. Okay, where do you go from here?"

"I don't know."

"There's always the morning after pill."

I shoot her a look and she raises her hands in defense.

"It's an option." Her voice softens, and I realize she's only trying to help.

"I know and sane individuals would have no qualms running to the drugstore, but..." I shake my head and let out a grunt. "Why did he ever enter my life?"

As soon as those words left my mouth, I knew they were a lie. Not for one minute have I ever regretted our relationship.

"I understand, but despite all the turbulence"—she stands to turn the griddle on when sounds of little feet padding across the hardwood floor fill the air—"would you really go back and change anything?"

The kids stumble into the kitchen and gather around me for hugs. Their voices mesh together in mouse-squeak harmony as each one vies for my attention. I peer into their groggy, sleepy-filled eyes and smile. "No. Not at all."

CHAPTER TWELVE

ZACH

FIVE YEARS AGO

"MR. ZACH PRITCHETT. OFFICIAL PITCHER FOR THE PHILLIES." Lacey holds up my Philadelphia Phillies baseball cap they gave me with a smile stretched from ear to ear.

"Technically the Lehigh Valley IronPigs." I secure the tape on the cardboard flaps and place the box next to the others. I shove a stick of gum in my mouth, pivot, and then pad across my bedroom floor to stand next to her.

"Nah, you negotiated a contract with the Phillies. That's a rare feat for someone straight out of college. You won't be in triple A for long. I'm so proud of you, Zach."

I swallow down any remorse our future holds and try to bask in her words. Our time together has run its course. She leaves in two days for her internship, and my parents—who couldn't be bothered with simple things like graduation—hired a mover to load my belongings. They come tomorrow morning. Tonight is all Lacey and I have left with each other, and we're stuck packing. Removing the hat from her hand, I force a smile and place it on her head.

"Keep it. It looks rather sexy on you."

The corners of her eyes crinkle as her smile softens. Fuck, I'm going to miss her. I redirect my attention to another box.

"I..."

She doesn't finish her sentence. Her eyes darken, sending impulses straight to my cock. I want tonight to be more than sex between us, but I really don't want to leave my room. What I want is to savor every inch of her body. Sear it into memory. Not that it isn't already. The regret of leaving her behind is already creeping through me, making me second-guess everything I've worked to achieve, but I need to be strong. All of my focus must be directed toward pitching, or I'll never make it.

"Zach, kiss me."

Her words zap me from my stance, and I realize I've been staring at her this whole time. But not now. I reach down and plant my lips to her mouth. Her fingers weave through my hair as I start out slow, worshiping every piece of her plump, lower lip. Her mouth opens, offering herself to me, but I continue my salacious assault. In no way am I rushing this evening.

I've never told her I love her. Even though I do, I didn't want to complicate things further. It's hard enough to leave her, but I'll be crushed if I hear those words said back to me.

My hands slip to the hem of that sexy scoop-neck Henley that's been teasing me with her soft tits all day. I slowly work the shirt above her head. The hat falls to the ground, but we're both too preoccupied at the moment to care. I walk her backward, my fingers fumbling with her bra until the backs of her knees touch the mattress. Once her bra joins the hat on the floor, I lower my gaze to her perfect-sized tits. The bulge against my zipper tightens, and I can't help myself. I lower my head and flick her nipple with my tongue while palming her breast. She's a perfect fit. I lift with a popping sound and stare into those heated eyes.

"Let's get these shorts off." I undo the top button, and the zipper flies open. I take both hands along her hips and scoot the jean material and underwear over her curves until she's standing in front of me completely naked. I can't believe I have to say goodbye to this beautiful, perfect girl.

I kiss along her neck as she removes my cargo shorts. They slide off easily enough, and we're not able to keep our hands off each other. I want to go slow, take my time. Drink her in. But my dick throbs so much I need to be inside her.

I push her back onto the bed, and we fall, hands gliding all over each other, legs intertwined. I can't stop kissing her.

Our tongues collide. I come up for a quick breath only to land my mouth on Lacey's neck and then work back to reclaim her tongue. I spread her legs apart and run my finger along her slick folds. She's so ready for me. Our last night. I don't want this to end.

"Zach—"

I cut her off with my mouth again and push my finger inside her. Her moan vibrates through my entire body. Fuck. Why does this have to end?

I position myself at her entrance.

"Zach—"

"Lacey," I moan as I enter her tight canal. Jesus, this feels great. Why does this feel so great? "I fucking love you."

She relaxes further at my words as she succumbs to the sensations flowing between us. I drive into her inch by inch as pleasure rolls through her eyes. I'm so close, but she's nowhere near ready. I put my greedy needs first and didn't have time to warm her up properly. I slow my pace, savoring in her tightness wrapped around me. God, I love being inside her pussy. This girl stole my heart a long time ago, and it only seems right when I'm in her.

Knowing she needs a bit more stimulus, I press my thumb over her clit and work in circles. Her eyes close as she arches her back, her beautiful breast inches from my mouth. I bite down on her nipple while quickening my pace. Her moan vibrates through me. I thrust deeper and deeper, working her clit as spasms of pleasure race through her. She's so damn sexy.

"That's it, baby. Come for me."

A sweet moan escapes her mouth, and by the tiny spasms coursing through her body, I know it won't be long. I grit my teeth to buy more time. A few minutes later, she clamps on my dick and writhes beneath me. I lose control and explode, spilling inside her.

It isn't until I slide out that I realize my mistake. *Shit.*

"Um ... babe."

"That's what I was trying to tell you," she says between pants.

I lie next to her and curl her by my side.

"You're on the pill, right?" How do I not know if she's on the pill? This entire month I've been inside her, I never thought to ask? I've always been conscientious. Not once have I ever been careless.

"It's okay," she says in a small voice. "I'll be fine."

Not exactly a yes, but I trust her. I intertwine our fingers together and bring them up to my mouth. I plant a kiss across her knuckles and sigh. "I don't want to leave tomorrow."

"I don't want you to leave." A beat of silence passes, and she quietly asks, "Are you okay?"

I tip my head toward her, unsure of what she's referring to. I'm not okay with a lot of stuff, but admission is hard to come by. "Now that's a loaded question."

She peers up at me, those green eyes laced with concern. "I mean, are you okay that your parents never came."

I shrug. "I won't lie. It stings a little that a bottle of beer means more to my parents than their son's graduation. But I wasn't surprised. I half-expected them to not show. So, yeah ... I'm okay with them."

"I'd share mine with you if I could."

"I wish it was that simple." I let go of her hand and trace my fingers along her soft skin. Damn, I don't want this night to end. Lacey doesn't mention a word about my confession of love that slipped out, but her lack of returning the sentiment doesn't go unnoticed. In truth, she doesn't have to voice the words aloud. I know she loves me. The way she looks at me is telling in itself, but when she melts against me, there's no denying her love. That's what makes this so hard.

She runs her hand across my pecs, and the soft kiss above my heart awakens my dick. We proceed to make love again, and this time I take my time. It's slow and sensual. Perfect. Even with knowing once morning comes I'll be making the biggest mistake of my life.

CHAPTER THIRTEEN

LACEY

CURRENT DAY

I PLACE THE THIN, SMALL PLATE AND MATCHING CUP INTO THE dishwasher. Even though I didn't eat much of Jocelyn's huge break-fast, my appetite has yet to return. It's one in the afternoon, and there's so much work that needs to be done. My article about athletes continuing to play while injured needs polishing. Honestly, I think my boss is trying to test my professional writing skills. Paired with the endless amount of housework, my day is booked. My problem? I have zero ambition.

I step toward the living room and flip the overhead fluorescent light off. Pausing, I turn and double-check if I placed the lunch meat in the refrigerator. The golden Formica countertops, marred with years of abuse from previous tenants, catch my eye. The entire kitchen needs to be updated, but that is certainly not in this year's budget. Or the next five. My small townhouse may be old and worn, but it's decent. The district I live in isn't the best, but the rent's affordable. To me, that means a lot, considering my slow start after college.

But I'm in a good spot now, even with the seventies color

scheme, which serves as a reminder of my less than decent behavior last night.

Last night.

That hole I wanted to crawl into this morning still tempts me, but the sex was worth it. I'm not a one-night-stand type of girl. Never have been—kind of the reason behind my recent dry spell—but being with Zach seemed more than a one-time fling. Even though that's exactly what last night was. It can't be anything more. The familiarity of being with Zach is how I'm justifying my actions.

Good sex trumps bad decisions. Period.

But I only think this way with Zach. I'm not lying when I say no other man can bring me to that level of ecstasy. It's practically sinful what Zach's dick can perform. He's *that* good. But there's no excuse for my lack of responsibility.

I mean really. What the heck was I thinking? When I confessed my actions to Jocelyn, I left a few details out. Like the part where he took me back to his hotel room. I'm so weak. When he told me he never screwed anyone but me without protection, the parade of blondes danced through my head. I felt used again. Pair those feelings with my stupidity for having unprotected sex, and it's no wonder I became withdrawn. But Zach homed in on my emotions, just as he always had, and sucked me right into the Zach Zone. I swear it's a real phenomenon. By the time he finished talking, I had swooned and was convinced to go back to his hotel with him.

But talk about embarrassment when we walked into the elegant lobby of the Grand Hyatt. My frayed, wrinkled dress, smeared makeup, and that just-fucked frizzy hair gave little to the imagination as to what we'd done. The disdainful look the lady in the elevator gave me made me feel like Julia Roberts in *Pretty Woman*. I almost asked if she wanted to watch.

But this isn't the movies. There's no Prince Charming riding up in a limo to come rescue me. In fact, I haven't given Zach my phone number nor do I have his. I mean, sure, there are ways he can get a hold of me, but now that he's had a taste of me, I'm sure he'll be done. And since I snuck away this morning before he woke up, my hint should be loud and clear.

I lean down and pick up the T-shirt I stole from his suitcase. I clutch it to my chest and inhale the faint scent of spice and musk.

Leaving this morning wasn't much better. Not with having to do the "walk of shame" through the hallways of the Grand Hyatt. Yeah, that happens all the time, right? Who knows, maybe it does. I really have no idea.

I do know one thing, though. I certainly couldn't wear the same clothes home. Jocelyn's dress was ruined. So, I did what I had to do. I stole the T-shirt, along with a pair of black sweats. High heels and sweats. A great combination. And even though my legs are long, the pants dwarfed me. I had to roll the waistband several times to keep them from falling. The debate is still out on whether that look was better than the wrinkled, frayed dress.

I sigh. At least, my curls were tamed by a hair tie.

As mortifying as everything was, the sex more than made up for it. I'm still sore, but as the tingles currently shooting south suggest, I want more. Zach brought me to orgasm three more times. And each time was unprotected. I'm such an idiot. It's like I played Russian roulette but with my vagina.

In all honesty, it's not like I could demand he sheath up after I lied about being on the pill, and it was too late anyway. His little swimmers were already inside me. I just don't know if they will lead to pregnancy.

Shit.

I know! I'll claim Catholicism and say I'm practicing the rhythm method. It hasn't been that long since my last period. Uh... bad idea. Don't those families have like five to eight kids or some-thing? I quickly count the days since my last period. Ten ... eleven ... right on the edge of ... *fuck*! I'm totally screwed.

I let out a puff of air and plop onto the couch, Zach's shirt still clutched in my hands. Perhaps I am stubborn and should get my butt to the pharmacy. Wouldn't that be the smartest choice? I glance down my hallway, and tears spring to my eyes. No, whatever happens, I'll deal.

The doorbell rings as soon as my phone buzzes. *Who the heck could be here?* Picking up my phone, my eyes narrow at the unknown number. *And who the heck is this?* I ignore the cell, spring from the couch, and beeline to the door. As I swing the door open in a rush, I can't stop my gasp.

Oh no.

I sneak another quick glance down the hallway before returning to the one person who should never be standing on my stoop.

Ever.

CHAPTER FOURTEEN
ZACH

CURRENT DAY

I wasn't sure what to expect when Lacey opened the door. I thought it might be her bright smile that lights up the entire room, that seductive stare that sends tingles straight to my dick, or her satiated, I've-been-fucked-hard-and-am-completely-satisfied look she gets after I've had my way with her. Any of those combinations flitted through my mind. But this scared, pale-faced, what-the-hell-is-he-doing-here expression isn't at all what I imagined. Maybe I shouldn't have sent the Uber driver away.

"Hey," I say, half-grinning.

Her gaze slides to her left and then back to me.

"Zach? What are doing here? Don't you have to get ready for the game?"

Okay, this clearly isn't at all how I'd hoped this meeting would go. I'm beginning to wonder if there's another guy in the house. But Lacey wouldn't go on a date with me if she was seeing someone else. People change throughout the years, but their morals usually stay the same.

"It's an evening game, remember. I have a few hours before

needing to check in." Standing on the pitted concrete stoop, I shift my weight, not missing the fact she hasn't invited me in. Why hasn't she invited me inside? There's no denying the connection we had with each other last night. By the way her body shuddered against mine, I know she enjoyed herself. I thought we rekindled the relationship I ruined. Was it just one-sided? I sure hope the hell not.

"Oh. Well, I uh..."

"Can I come inside to talk?"

"Um ... now isn't really a good time."

"Okay. I can come back later tonight..." I let my sentence die because we both know it would be closer to midnight by the time I would get here. Neither one of us wants that, but I'm not leaving town without talking to her.

Lacey's hesitation confuses me even more. I open my mouth to call her out on it but snap it shut when she steps aside. Taking full advantage, I barrel forward and enter a dated but decent enough home. She's added her touch to the decor. It's warm and inviting, just like her. I turn and close the distance between us. Her eyes widen as if I'm intimidating her. Where'd my sexy seductress from last night go?

"You left before we could talk."

"I had things I needed to do."

"Bullshit. I think you ran away, scared."

Her chin juts up, and that fiery look crosses her eyes. There's the Lacey I know.

"I'm not scared of you. Of this." She waves her hand back and forth between us. "What exactly do you think is going on, Zach?"

I don't offer an explanation because what I want is more long-term than she's obviously ready for. Instead, I drag my phone out of my pocket and pull up her contact information I added this morning. Everything, that is, except her number. When I switched phones years ago, I intentionally didn't add her. I didn't want to fight the temptation of calling her. But the omission never did any good. Those digits were filed deep into memory along with every inch of her body.

"What's your phone number?"

"You came all the way here for my number?"

My lips twitch. "How else am I supposed to get a hold of you?"

She sighs but rattles off the numbers, my fingers hovering over the digits for a moment. "That's the same number as in college."

"Yep. There was never a reason to change."

Son of a bitch. I could've called her all this time.

"Why do you want it now?" she asks.

I stare at her, wondering what changed from last night. She's so nervous, and it's apparent she wants me gone.

"I finally found you again and don't want this to end like the last time. We deserve another chance to make this work." So much for being subtle.

"What? You see me from afar, and now you're suddenly in love with me? Do you know how crazy that sounds? You're a freaking baseball player, for crying out loud."

"How the hell does my career have anything to do with the fact I've always loved you?" I peer directly into her eyes. "I may have left you back in college, but I loved you, and I never stopped."

The fight leaves her expression, and although I can tell she wants to believe me, she doesn't. She's so damn guarded. What has her so bottled up? I never planned on having to find a way to convince her.

Lacey huffs and sidesteps around me. She retreats to the couch where she gathers what looks like my shirt and sweats. Her shoulders slump forward as she stands there, clutching the clothes. For a moment, I think she's going to hurl around and toss them at me, demanding I leave, but she just stands there in a defeated stance. I walk up behind her and place my hands on her shoulders.

"Babe, I'm not lying. I've always loved you. I've just been too stupid to act on it."

"You need to leave. I'm not sure what you're thinking, but we don't have a future together."

Pain jolts through my chest. What changed between last night and now? Her actions yesterday left little doubt that she's still in love with me. I sensed it. But now, she's determined to push me away. I don't understand.

I clamp my jaw tight as I look toward the ceiling. I need to calm down before I say something to worsen the situation. Trying to focus on something else, I scan the tiny living room and land on a pink princess toy chest. Confusion crosses my mind. She admitted to not talking to her family. If that's the case, why have toys for her nieces? I start looking at the bookshelves lined with various pictures of a young girl. The same girl with long curly hair. Holy shit.

"Do you have a kid?" I blurt out half-surprised, half-hurt that this is how I'm finding out. Does she not trust me enough to have told me she has a daughter?

Lacey stiffens beneath my hands, and I have my answer as to why she's trying to avoid me. She thinks I wouldn't be interested in her if she's a mother. She doesn't trust me. But she couldn't be farther from the truth.

"Zach, you need to leave. Now!"

"I'm not going anywhere until you talk to me. It doesn't matter if you have a child." I spin her around and force her to look at me. "I'm in love with you, regardless."

Tears well in her eyes, but she's shaking her head.

"Please leave."

"I'm not going anywhere until we talk this out."

"There's nothing to talk about. Nothing is going on between us."

"Mommy?" The sweetest voice rings through the air.

Both of our heads turn to a little girl standing at the hallway's entrance. We both gasp. Lacey's out of fright; mine out of shock. I immediately drop my hands from Lacey's shoulders and step backward. The temperature heats up a few degrees while the room spins as I stare into the deep blue eyes of a little angel.

Lacey sighs, but I don't move; my eyes are fixated on the little girl.

"It's okay, honey. Come say hi to Mommy's friend."

Little feet tromp across the worn carpet. With each closer step, I feel as if I've been gut-punched. And the safe distance she maintains from me magnifies the blow.

"How old is she?" I ask, trying to keep the panic out of my voice. But I'm anything but calm. Inside I'm boiling mad because I already know the answer.

The girl hugs Lacey's legs and stares at me. Lacey remains tight-lipped.

"How old?" I say through gritted teeth.

After a beat, the little blonde wiggles four fingers. "I'm four."

Lacey snaps out of her funk. She bends down and picks her up. The air thickens, and I can hardly breathe as I look at the girl. *My girl.* She has to be.

"You're a beautiful four-year-old," I somehow manage to squeeze out.

"Who are you?" she asks, her little nose scrunched.

My gaze snaps to Lacey who looks as frightened as I feel. I don't know what to say. I want to say I'm your father, but I don't have confirmation yet. And who the fuck blurts "I'm your father" in real life?

"Sweetie, could you go to your room? I'll be there in a bit. I just need to say a few words to my friend Zach."

I flinch at the *friend* wordage.

"I just woke up." The little girl sticks her slightly larger lower lip into a pout, and a piece of my heart shatters. She may have the same eyes as me, but her mouth is all her momma's.

"I know, honey, but you can get the Play-Doh down, and we'll create some pieces of art."

"All right!" She squirms out of Lacey's arms and hightails it to her bedroom. As soon as she rounds the corner, I whip my head back to Lacey.

"Is she mine?" I blurt, not able to control the anger in my voice.

Lacey swallows hard as tears return to her pretty green eyes. "Yes."

The room begins to spin again as her confirmation drives home. I'm a father? I take a step toward the hallway but pause as Lacey grabs my arm.

"Please wait. Let me explain you to her first."

"I want to see her."

"Please, Zach. Come back tomorrow, and I promise you can meet her. I'll explain everything to her."

I take a calming breath. If I don't relax, I'll end up yelling and making my little girl afraid of me. I turn back toward Lacey.

"Why didn't you tell me I had a daughter?" I step away, needing some distance. "Jesus, Lacey. Why would you keep her from me?"

"It's not like that. I wanted to tell you. There were so many nights that I picked up the phone and tried to call, but I couldn't. You were just getting started with your career. By the time I got enough courage, your number had changed. I didn't try anymore because you didn't need this distraction."

"Distraction?" I yell and then lower my voice. "What the hell, Lacey? She's my kid."

"I know and believe me, I'm so sorry, but that time in my life was confusing. We'd just broken up, and I'd started that intern job. Five weeks into my internship, I found out I was pregnant. I tried to tell you, but … no, it doesn't matter. I just didn't know what to do."

"Letting me know I was a father would've been the best choice. Why wouldn't you tell me? I could've been there for you."

"Would you? You *left* me, Zach. You chose baseball over me, so what was I to think?"

"I loved you, damn it."

"Really, Zach? Because I remember things differently. Did you know I went to see you?" She clamps her mouth shut as if she didn't mean to admit that.

"What do you mean?"

"Nothing, I—"

"What did you mean?" I ask harsher.

"Fine, if you really want to know. I flew down to Florida where you were playing. Believe me, I had every intention of telling you, but this had to be told in person."

She came down to visit me? In Florida? My stomach tightens. "When?"

"Does it matter?"

"Yes, it matters. When?"

Tears spring to her eyes, and the tiny shiver that shakes her shoulders makes me want to hold her. Protect her. But I'm so damn mad I can't think straight.

"The end of August," she murmurs.

Shit.

And because I am a masochist, I have to ask, "Why didn't you talk to me?"

"Because you had already moved on. I wasn't going to come between you and your *friend.*"

I could feel myself pale. She has to be referring to the cleat chaser I took home. It was only that one night. Fuck, I knew screwing that girl was a mistake.

"I'm so sorry you had to see that." I step closer to her.

"Save it." She puts her hands up to stop me.

"You need to understand. I wasn't in a good place during that time. I—"

She huffs. "Good place? Do you think *I* was in a good place? I spent the whole summer missing you. I was miserable without you. Then to find out that you used me the whole time."

"I *never* used you, Goddamn it. I loved you. What? You don't think I was miserable?"

"Three months, Zach. That's all it took before you stuck your dick into someone else. It took me"—she breaks into a sob—"it took me over a year."

Remorse punches my gut. I don't even know what to say, but

I'm so pissed at her, and everything is a blur. I'm certainly not thinking straight.

"I truly am sorry you had to see that, but you should've told me."

"After I had come back home, I was going to, but like I said, you turned off your phone."

I'm a fucking idiot. "There were other ways of getting hold of me. I would've come back."

"And what? Throw away your promising career? I couldn't let that happen."

"I could've still played."

"Yeah, but your head wouldn't have been in it."

I run my hands through my hair and let out a frustrated groan. She's right. Between juggling baseball and dealing with my parents, this would've broken me. But damn it, she's my kid. I had every right to know.

"What ... what's her name?"

Lacey closes her eyes and takes a deep breath as if to calm herself. What can be so bad about a name? Did she name her something stupid? Anger begins to boil again.

"Zoe," she whispers.

My body stiffens as a sudden coldness hits my core. I shuffle back a step or two, creating a much-needed distance. Hearing Zoe's name is like another punch to the stomach.

"You named her Zoe?" I ask, barely audible.

"At the time, I thought it'd be appropriate." Tears spill down her cheek. "I can tell now that was wrong."

"No, it's just..." I let my words die, not knowing what else to say.

"I guess I wanted a piece of you attached to her."

"I'm glad you did. It's a noble gesture." I take a step toward Lacey. "Thanks. I just ... another Zoe Pritchett."

"Uh..." Lacey bites her lip, and I can tell she's contemplating something else.

"Spit it out."

"It's not ... Zoe's not..."

"Just say it," I demand.

"Zoe's last name isn't Pritchett. It's Stark.

What the hell? Her words rekindle the fire brewing inside me.

"You gave my daughter your last name?"

"I couldn't risk you finding out, so I listed father unknown. I'm so sorry."

"Jesus, Lacey. Her last name is the first thing I'm changing." I step toward the hallway again, determined to see Zoe. Consequences be damned.

"Please, I beg you. Let me talk to her first. Then if you want to come back tomorrow or the next time you're in town, then—"

"The next time I'm in town?" I whip around to face her. "Do you think I can walk away?"

"That's not what I meant. I know you wouldn't walk away. That's why I never told you back then."

"You still should've told me," I yell.

"Don't blame this all on me. I can bear most of the blame, but you're not completely innocent in this. You fucked me without a condom and never once thought about the consequences. I didn't receive one phone call asking if I was okay. In fact, you never called at all."

I rear back as if I've been slapped. Fuck, she's right. I never gave one thought about whether she'd end up pregnant or not. And I never called because it hurt too much to talk to her. I knew I'd crawl back to her if I broke down and dialed her number.

"We never fucked. You always meant more to me than that. *Shit!* Maybe I should've stepped up and followed through, but it never occurred to me then." Damn, I am an asshole. How could I have not considered the consequences? I run my hand through my hair again and let it rest on my neck. "You still should've told me."

"I wanted to. Believe me, I wanted to." Lacey sounds defeated. With a sigh, she backs toward the couch and sits. "I was so angry and hurt, and I knew a baby was the last thing you needed to concentrate on. So, I chose not to tell you."

"That wasn't your decision to make."

"I know. But I was young and starting my own career. I did what I thought was best for everyone."

I study Lacey for a moment. Keeping this inside her has taken its toll. I can see the worry lines frame her face. I'm not blind. But we spent an entire evening together last night, and she never once brought up the fact she has a child.

"That explains the first couple of years, but what about now? Zoe's four years old. Did you ever plan on telling me?"

I swallow down the pain that surfaces when Zoe's name is mentioned. Although it came as a shock, I love the fact she named her after my sister. When my anger subsides, I'll have to tell Lacey how much I appreciate the gesture.

Lacey sags farther into the couch and closes her eyes. My chest tightens, and I remind myself not to console her. I want to wrap her in my arms and tell her everything's going to be okay, but damn it, it's not okay. I've lost four years with Zoe. And what makes it worse? My own daughter doesn't even know me. Hell, she looked frightened of me.

"No," Lacey admits.

The last piece of my heart breaks as my jaw clamps tight. I nod and pivot toward the front door. "My lawyer will be in touch."

CHAPTER FIFTEEN

ZACH

CURRENT DAY

I SWIRL THE GOLDEN NECTAR AROUND THE GLASS BEFORE TAKING a sip. Tonight calls for something stronger than beer. I still don't like to drink much during the season, but tonight's an exception. Tonight, I'm getting drunk. After all, that's what the Pritchett men do best, right? Shocking news occurs ... get drunk.

AJ and a few teammates occupy a corner booth, but I'm not up for socializing. My ass perched on this barstool suits me just fine.

"It must be pretty bad for you to be hitting the hard stuff," Jax says. He slaps a hand on my back and then sits beside me at the bar. "I must admit. After last night, I thought you'd be in a better mood."

I grunt, barely acknowledging his presence. He knew who I was with last night, so his comment comes as no surprise.

"Just keeping up the family tradition." I raise the glass and take a swig.

"Man, AJ wasn't exaggerating when he complained about your foul ass mood. What the hell happened between you and Lacey?"

I study the amber liquid and with the slightest movement,

shake my head. Where do I even begin? No one knows my history with Lacey better than Jax. Hell, after Lacey and I broke up, he listened to my endless whine sessions. He never once agreed with my decision, but he respected me enough to offer sympathy. That is, if "you're a dumbass" is considered consoling.

"Last night," I say with a huff. "If you'd seen me this morning, I would've told you it was like old times. Those suppressed feelings for Lacey resurfaced with a vengeance." I take a swig of my whiskey and plop the glass down a little too hard. Aware of how wimpy I'm sounding. "But after I went to visit her this afternoon ... it was as if I've never known her."

Jax's eyes darken with confusion, but he remains quiet. The good friend he is, he waits for an explanation as I plan my next words. There's no way he's more confused than me. Never in a million years would I ever suspect Lacey capable of being dishonest, but that's what this feels like—complete betrayal.

"Turns out, the reason behind Lacey's reluctance to meet me was a huge secret she never intended for me to find out."

"What do you mean? Don't tell me she's seeing someone else. I mean, I'm surprised she's not married, but..."

I wince and toss back the last of my drink. Motioning for a refill, I set the empty glass back down and turn toward Jax.

"Apparently, I have a daughter."

I should've waited for Jax to swallow his drink because the second my words spill out, so does his beer.

"What?" he sputters.

"Yeah. I have the cutest little four-year-old daughter you'll ever see."

"Holy fuck." Jax takes a swig of his beer and readjusts his shirt. "How? I mean ... why? I mean ... what the hell are you going to do?"

"I don't know. I've missed four years of her life. Fuck, I'm still missing out. She doesn't even know me."

"You need to be with them. Take tomorrow off. If you talk to the coach, I'm sure he'll under—"

Two tall, slender girls interrupt Jax as they flank our sides.

"You look like you could use some cheering up." The girl flips her long, auburn hair to the side and leans closer to me. Running her hand along my arm, she lowers her voice as she says, "I bet I can bring a smile to your face."

I study the girl for a second. Her beautiful hair coloring, the hopefulness in her jade-colored eyes, and her sexy, seductive smile are attributes I prefer in a woman, but only with one woman. There's a reason I've only dated bleach blonde women since my split from Lacey. Gingers serve too much as a reminder, and brunettes are too related to the auburn color. But even if this girl were the hottest blonde on earth, I still wouldn't be interested. Not after being with Lacey again.

I shift away as my dick twitches from the simple thought of Lacey. Damn, that girl ruined me. There's no denying the sex between us is hot, but she's also the only girl I've ever connected with. In truth, the only one I want underneath me, but I can't think that way. Not with all this anger swirling through my veins. I'm not quite sure I'll ever get over this rage.

I glance at the temptress currently staking a claim. I'd tell her that I'm taken, but some women find that as a challenge. And I'm in no mood to mess with her.

"I'm sure you could if I was interested, but I'm not feeling it tonight. Besides, I was in the middle of a conversation with my friend." I turn to Jax and frown. He has his hand planted on the brunette's ass. She's pressed up against him with her hand resting on his inner thigh, slowly stroking.

Really?

That guy is a bonafide horndog. I don't need to deal with this shit now.

"Your friend looks like he's enjoying himself." She runs her fingers on my arm again.

"Sorry, honey. It's not happening tonight."

She pouts, and Zoe's lower lip springs to mind. I'm totally fucked. Not only do women remind me of Lacey, but now they're reminding me of Zoe. But unlike this chick's, Zoe's pout was cute. Adorable even.

"At least be a gentleman and buy me a drink," she purrs.

The low growl vibrates through my chest as I motion for the bartender. Reaching for my wallet, I shoot Jax a glare. He must take in my expression because he unwinds himself from the girl.

"Sorry, sweetheart. Maybe later. I need to talk to my friend right now."

"Aw, you're such a good friend." She strokes his cock through his jeans and adds, "Later, I can show you what a good savior I can be."

For fuck's sake. Does this chick realize how corny she sounds?

"Get these girls whatever they want and keep the rest." I shove the fifty-dollar bill into the bartender's hand. That should take care of them for a while.

As soon as the girls get their drinks, they shuffle away, giggling. I turn to Jax, who's eyeing the brunette's sweet ass.

"What the hell, bro? Can't you keep it in your pants long enough to have a simple conversation?"

"Ha, ha. At least I wrap mine. No one can claim a paternity suit on me. Yet, anyway."

My face pales, and I close my eyes. "Fuck," I mutter.

"Sorry, too soon?"

"No. It's just ... I didn't use a condom last night."

The mindless chatter and clinking of glasses escalate as Jax's silence screams volumes. I open an eye and glance at him. The slack-jawed expression makes me grimace.

"I knew you were a dumbass, but I thought Lacey was at least smart."

"She is smart, asshole."

It's apparent I'm not. No, I'm a fucking idiot. She said she was on the pill, didn't she? It doesn't matter. I'm not making the same mistake twice. I'll be damn sure to follow up this time.

A picture of the three of us walking together with another baby growing inside Lacey flits through my mind. We're hand in hand with Zoe in the middle. The image is so vivid I can visualize their smiles. It should scare the hell out of me, but it doesn't. Instead, fucking warm fuzzies fill my chest, and I want nothing more than to make that vision a reality. I need to squash those feelings. That scenario will not happen. Not with knowing I missed out on Zoe's first step, first words, first everything. I can't admit that to Jax though. I'm already acting like a pussy.

"Like I said, I'm sure the coach will give you a personal day tomorrow. You don't pitch until Tuesday."

"I already talked to him. He was cool with giving me the time off. First thing in the morning, I'm going to Lacey's home and meeting my daughter, Zoe."

"Zoe?" Jax raises an eyebrow. "She named your daughter after your sister?"

"Yeah."

"No wonder it hit you hard."

Yeah, because finding out I'm a father isn't shocking enough. Asshole. "It's actually a nice gesture."

"I do like that she honored your sister. And Zoe Pritchett has a nice ring to it."

"It would if that was her last name," I quip, my anger resurfacing.

Jax flinches from my harsh tone.

"Ouch. Sorry, man. I just assumed."

"Don't worry. I *will* get that changed." A low moan rumbles from me. "Jesus, I threatened her with a lawyer."

"To get the name changed? That should be easy."

"No, for custody." A pang of guilt throat punches me from the devastated look on Lacey's face. There's no way in hell I could obtain custody.

"Is that what you want?" Jax stares at me as if I've lost my mind. Maybe I have.

"No. I mean, I'd love for her to live with me, but there's no way. Not with all the away games we play. Besides, she doesn't know me. I could never take her away from her mother."

He takes another drink and shakes his head.

"I fucking love her, but what she did? I'll never forgive her for this."

"Give it time, dude. I'm not trying to defend Lacey's choices, but look at it from her perspective. Four years ago, you couldn't handle baseball and a relationship. I'm not surprised she didn't tell you right away, but—"

"She did try, once." The last thing I want to do is bring up the Florida trip, but I can't have Jax thinking she never tried. That wouldn't be fair to Lacey.

"What do you mean?"

"Remember when you yelled at me to find a piece of ass to get over her?"

His face pales as he nods.

"You know that I listened, and apparently, Lacey saw her leaving my apartment."

"Fuck."

"Yeah, she flew down to tell me in person—it's not like she could've told me over the phone since I changed my number—but she overheard me telling my 'goodbye' spiel to the cleat chaser."

"Jesus, Zach. Had I known, I never would've given you that advice."

"It's not your fault. I own that deceit."

He winces and tosses back his drink. "I don't know what to say, buddy. If she had told you, do you honestly believe you would've handled becoming a daddy?"

"Maybe not, but I'll never know. Will I?"

CHAPTER SIXTEEN
LACEY

CURRENT DAY

"What time is Zach coming over?" Jocelyn asks.

When my heart rate felt as if it would burst from my ribcage, I called my best friend yesterday after Zach left. Jocelyn has been there for me since the beginning of my pregnancy. She was the only person I could rely on. Still is today, which is apparent by her early morning phone call.

"Eleven. He can only stay for a few hours because he needs to board the plane by five. The team flies to Chicago." I curl my legs underneath me and settle onto the couch. Zoe's asleep, and I'm taking full advantage of my alone time.

"How did Zoe take the news?"

I let out a humorless laugh.

"Better than me. Even though she was skittish when they initially met, she became so excited after I explained who he was. The little squirt surprises me, but then again, she's always wanted a daddy. Telling her went way better than expected."

"This is a good thing. It's about time he found out. That they both found out. But you knew my opinion on that subject from day one."

"Yeah, and you're right. I'm glad it's finally out in the open." That's the partial truth. There's still part of me that's terrified.

"To add to my stress, I got asked out yesterday."

Turns out, the unknown caller I ignored when Zach showed up was Brayden. He left a voicemail asking me to call him back. Several hours passed before returning that call. Procrastination could be blamed as well. I was ninety-nine percent sure that his intent was to ask me out, and I wasn't mistaken. The last thing I need now is to date some random guy.

"What? By who?"

"Brayden Hicks. He works for CBS New York. I met him at the post press conference."

"Holy shit. After a five-month dry spell, two guys start chasing you? What did you say?"

"What could I say? I turned him down." I grumbled. "Maybe I should've told him I have baby daddy drama. That would've scared him away." Hell, I don't need to add the drama part. Most guys check out once they find out I gave birth.

"Do you *want* to go out with him?"

"Not really. He's nice and cute, but…"

"I know." Jocelyn lets out a long, dramatic sigh. "He's no Mr. Fucking Specialist, Zach."

"More like, Mr. Ruin You For Life From Every Other Guy." My face reddens, but I stand by my earlier admission. The guy can fuck. I release a whiny groan. "What am I going to do? He's going to hate me for life."

"Well, you never wanted to get back with him, anyway. Right?"

"Right." I doubt my non-confident tone convinced her—it certainly didn't convince me—but there's no chance of reconciling with Zach. Not now and it stings something fierce. I lower my voice. "What am I going to do if he wants custody? I can't hire a fancy lawyer. I can't compete with his kind of money."

The biggest understatement of the year. I spring from the couch and start pacing a path in my already worn carpet.

"He's not going to take Zoe away from you."

"I'm not so sure. Zach's parting words mentioned a lawyer."

"He's upset. Understandably so. Let him calm down, and he'll realize what's in front of him."

"A four-year-old daughter that doesn't know him and a woman who lied to him?"

"No, a chance at starting the family he subconsciously wants."

"I doubt that. You didn't see Zach when he left. He was pissed." I pinch the bridge of my nose, in desperate need of calming down. "God, he'll hate me for life."

"No, he won't. I may not have seen Zach for years, but you'd have to be a moron to not know he still loves you. Once he calms down, he'll realize how great this can be."

"I'm the biggest moron, and I disagree with you. This is too big. This is 'I slept with your brother' type big. He's not going to forgive me."

"But that's what you want, right?"

I groan.

"I *knew* you wanted him back!"

"No, I don't."

"You're only lying to yourself." She sighs when I don't answer. Then in a stern voice, she says, "Look, the benefits outweigh the loss, give it time."

"I suppose." I glance at the clock and cringe. I've run out of time. "As much as I hate to, I need to get Zoe ready. He'll be here soon, and she wants to look extra pretty for him."

"Aw, that's so sweet."

"Yeah, like I said, she's taking this way better than I ever expected."

"Good luck. You know I love you."

"Love you, too."

I disconnect the call and charge toward Zoe's room. Eleven o'clock can't come and go quick enough.

⬦

Technically, Zach and Zoe have already met, but that information does nothing to calm my jittery nerves. Zoe sits on the couch in her pink and white sundress. Her hair—a ringlet of natural curls—is pulled back at the sides, accented by a frilly bow. Her little words "I want to be pretty for Daddy so he'd like me" slice through my soul, and the determination etched on her face makes me want to cry. I shouldn't have denied her access to her father. No matter what pathetic excuse I used to justify my actions or how much he hurt me, it was still wrong.

The rapid knock on the door makes me jump. I swallow down my fear and walk to face the inevitable. Momentarily closing my eyes, I let out a huff of air while grabbing the door handle. My confidence restored, I swing the door open and greet him with a timid smile that falls flat when I take in his dark, grim expression.

Great. He won't even look at me. I was right. Zach hates me.

"Come on in," I say and step out of the way. "There's a park not too far away. I thought we could walk there. That way it'd be a neutral place for you."

Zach nods but says nothing. There's only one other time I've ever seen Zach be unsure of himself, and that was our last night we spent together. The last time I was with him. But his ill-stricken face leaves little doubt. He's scared shitless as he steps toward the couch.

Zoe stares up at him, her bright blue eyes shining and her small foot shaking. Zach crouches down in front of her.

"Hey, Zoe. You look beautiful today."

"Thank you. Are you my daddy? Mommy says you are."

"Yes, sweetheart."

Zach's voice croaks, and it feels as if an anvil is crushing my chest. I can hardly breathe. I have to clamp my teeth hard to stop the tears from forming.

Zoe's face scrunches as she studies Zach.

"Where's your cape?"

"My cape?"

"Yeah, silly." She rolls her eyes. "*All* superheroes have capes. Everyone knows this."

"You think I'm a superhero?"

"Yeah. Mommy called you a hero. She said people love you, and you helped them. That makes you a superhero."

Her tone is serious as she sits there with a *duh* expression. One day after preschool, she asked why the other kids had daddies, and she didn't. I had told her that Zach was a hero to a lot of people and they loved and depended on him. That was the reason he wasn't ever around. I had no idea she turned him into someone with extraordinary abilities.

"I told her that so long ago," I whisper.

Zach puffs out a breath and turns toward me. It's the first time he's fully acknowledged my presence, but that's not what pins me to my spot. His expression of gratitude mixes with a sense of awe as he appears so bewildered. It's as if he expected me to bash him like so many exes do. No matter how badly I wanted to hate him, I could never do that. Other than not following through with our careless night, he did nothing wrong. Technically, we were broken up when he slept with that girl. He blinks out of his daze, and the pit in my stomach churns when indifference masks his features again. He turns back to Zoe.

"I'm hoping to be your hero now. Would you like that?"

A huge grin breaks across Zoe's face, and she leans forward, wrapping her arms around him in a tight hug.

Zach pauses for a moment with his arms suspended as if he doesn't know what to do with them. He figures it out quickly and hugs her back with the same tenacity. His face draws tight, and my heart breaks from the anguish displayed in every curve.

"I promise to be a better dad," he says, voice cracking.

Zoe pats him on the back, consoling him. It's so freaking cute and sweet, the tears spill over. I swipe under my eyelids before Zach sees me.

"Did you want to go to the park?"

"Yes! I like the swings. You can push me like the other daddies." She hops off the couch and reaches for both our hands.

Zach says nothing as he wraps his large fingers around hers. A moment later, the three of us take off, side by side, to the park. Tension radiates off Zach as his gaze shifts side to side, scoping the surrounding neighborhood. He's uncomfortable as hell. It doesn't take a genius to figure that out. I don't live in the safest area, but it's not the worst either. It's conducive for my means, but that doesn't mean I'd take an evening stroll by myself.

As soon as the park is within sight, Zoe worms out of our grasps and bolts toward the swings. Zach runs his hand through his hair and rests it on his neck as he stares after her. I want to reach out to him. Touch him. But I can't. God, I hate this awkwardness between us.

"Despite my intentions, I knew in time you'd be a part of her life. I didn't want her to hate or fear you."

"I appreciate that." He turns to face me. "Look, I was angry yesterday. Not to mention a little shocked. I said some things I didn't mean. I have no intention of taking her away from you. I just want to be a part of her life. But I won't lie. It will be hard with my schedule." He blows out a breath. "You've done a great job raising her. I can see that."

"Thanks." We edge our way to the swings in silence. When I can't stand the quietness anymore, I ask, "Do you live in Philadelphia, then?"

"I have a small apartment in Central Rittenhouse Square, downtown Philadelphia."

"No expensive home in the suburbs?" I tease and watch Zoe settle onto the seat.

"Nah, I never knew where I'd settle." He shrugs and eyes the area again. "I will move you guys out of this neighborhood, though."

"What?" My head snaps toward him.

"I don't feel like this is a safe enough place for a single mother.

I don't want to worry about the safety of my daughter when I can't be around."

"I'm not letting you pay my rent, and I can't afford much more." I bristle.

"Why not? The way I see it, I owe you a shit load of back child support."

"You don't owe me anything."

"How's this? I find you somewhere safer, and I'll cover whatever the difference will be in rent."

I don't say anything because it's a great deal, and I know it. But he can't come into our lives and disrupt it like this. Moving is a large gesture.

"Daddy," Zoe yells. "Hurry up."

"I'm coming." He steps toward the swings but halts as he turns back to me. "You don't have to commit yet. But think it over."

"I will."

He trots toward Zoe, and I stare after him feeling perplexed. I wanted to ask about his shoulder pain, but he sidetracked me with talk about moving. Zach returning to my life will be very frustrating, I'm afraid.

CHAPTER SEVENTEEN

ZACH

CURRENT DAY

A CURSE FLIES FROM MY MOUTH AS I WATCH THE BALL SAIL TO middle field, hit the brick wall, and disappear into the infamous Wrigley Field ivy. The crowd erupts as the runner on third advances, spreading the deficit wider. The center field man immediately throws his hands up, and the umpire signals a ground-rule double. *Shit*. The run counts.

Trailing by three points with Chicago's ace on the mound, we have our work cut out for us. The once-anticipated pitcher's duel took a back seat when my world turned upside down three nights ago. Instead of matching his talent pitch by pitch, I proceeded to play the game like a rookie's debut in the majors. I can't fucking concentrate. Between the nagging pain in my shoulder and learning about my daughter, I'm a mess. Three days have passed since meeting her. She's so freaking adorable. I never knew that type of love existed. I loved her mother. Hell, I still do, but this type of love seems different. The problem? I can't get past this anger festering deep inside me. Lacey's betrayal has me so pissed I can't see straight. And it's not as if I'm completely innocent, but I can't seem to let it go.

I turn to face my catcher and groan at Coach McFay sprinting to the mound. It's only the third inning. If I leave now, that's two games I've left early this season. Two too many during a contract year. Who cares about the no-no. That'd be reduced to a fluke. What they'll analyze are the two games I left early.

"You pitched a hell of a game," McFay lies. The coach is known for maintaining a positive tone, but he's laying the bullshit rather thick. "Go to the locker room and have Tim examine you."

"I'm okay," I lie right back.

"Get checked out. We'll talk afterward."

I nod at the finalization in his voice. I step off the mound, and Gonzalez swats my butt. He's positioned better than anyone to analyze my mistakes. I can fool everyone else, but he knows every missed mark.

Not one teammate says a word to me when I arrive at the dugout. I grip my glove tightly, overcoming the urge to hurl it against the wall. Instead, I maintain my cool and head straight to the team locker room in search of Tim. It doesn't take long to find him and to learn another X-ray is in order.

The news about our loss breaks across my phone while I wait in the hospital waiting room for the MRI results. Talk about letting the team down today. Today's loss is all on me. The first item on my to-do list is to apologize to my teammates. I certainly didn't give my hundred percent.

I drop my head into my hands and rest my elbows on my legs. I don't care if anyone snaps a picture of me looking defeated. I pretty much am at this moment. And I would be lying if I didn't say I was scared shitless. If the doctor comes out and says "Torn rotator cuff," I don't know what I'll do. But one thing's for sure, I'm sick of shoulder problems plaguing my entire career.

An hour or so later, Coach McFay waltzes into the waiting room and clears his throat. I raise my head and meet his gaze. His frown as he motions me to follow doesn't settle well. My stomach still churns as he leads me to a private room where the doctor waits for us. When the doctor points toward the films and explains the results—a severe case of shoulder tendinitis—I breathe for the first time since leaving the mound. Another cortisone shot and rest to decrease the inflammation. That I can handle.

The doctor exits. I get ready to follow but halt at the sight of Coach's somber expression. *Shit! We're not done.*

"This is a perfect opportunity for you to take a few weeks off and go on the D.L. to regroup. Get to know your child, and then when you return, you'll be a force to be reckoned with." Coach rests his hand on my good shoulder. "Zach, you're a talented pitcher. One of the best I've had the privilege to coach. Take time off, and you'll come back stronger."

I contemplate what he says, not like I have much choice, but I need to think this through. I admit, getting to know my daughter sounds like the best plan at resting my shoulder. I can't wait for the time we're no longer strangers. Our FaceTime chats the past two evenings have been awkward. It'll be good to spend some quality time with her.

"This is the first time a major distraction has affected your pitching," Coach continues when I don't respond. "You've been lucky so far. You've been able to focus strictly on baseball, and you've excelled because of it."

"Lucky? I've lost four years with my daughter."

"Yeah. I know. But you have her now. Learn to embrace it."

I understand what he's saying, and a small part of me is glad to have accomplished what I had, but I believe I could've done that with a wife and child—no doubt, I would've married Lacey. *If that's true, then why did I let her go? Because I was stupid, that's why.*

CHAPTER EIGHTEEN

LACEY

CURRENT DAY

I STARE AT MY COMPUTER. THE WORDS FOR THE METS STORY ARE written, but they're not making sense. The chrome symbol stares at me from the bottom left corner, tempting me to click the sports page and listen to the Philly-Cubs game. Zach's pitching today, and the last thing I need is a constant reminder of him, but I'm dying to know if he's pitching well. I never got to ask him about his shoulder a few days ago, and I'm worried about him.

"Your golden boy is hurt."

My heart sinks as my gaze flits to my boss walking toward me.

"No," I say, dragging the word out.

"He left the bottom of the third inning with shoulder pain."

Tears well in my eyes. He must be devastated. My grandfather comes to mind and all the hurt and regret he went through. *Please don't let this be a career-ending injury.*

"Has the press release been given yet?"

"No. Rumor has it he's flying back to Philly." Larry leans in and deepens his tone. "This is your break. I want you on the first car out to Philly. Set up an interview and do an exclusive."

My eyes narrow at his less than innocent expression. As worried as I am, I suspect Larry is up to something.

"Okay, what gives? The *New York Times* is not *that* interested in Zach's shoulder." I figure we wiped out the travel budget with my last trip to San Diego: the behind-the-dugout tickets, staying at the five-star hotel, and not just any hotel, the same hotel as ... *sonofabitch*. "You knew the Phillies team would be staying at the same hotel as me. Didn't you?"

A smirk crosses his face. The jerk doesn't even have the decency to look guilty.

"I was doing my job." He shrugs. "I'm good at it."

"No, you knew I'd run into Zach. Why are you pushing his story on me?"

"Lacey, I'm getting ready to retire. Before I go, I want you settled."

"You're not my dad. You're my boss." I grimace at his hurtful expression. Larry's been more of a dad to me these past few years than my own father.

"I've watched you struggle with being a single parent, and you've done a wonderful job. But your excuses have run their course."

The sudden rush of adrenaline takes me by surprise. I slip my shaking hands under the desk and sit straighter.

"My excuses?"

"Yeah. Do you honestly believe I never knew?"

"Knew what?" Caution creeps into my tone.

He sighs and gives me a look. "It's high time that little girl of yours knows her daddy."

The room creates a vacuum and sucks every drop of air from my lungs. I'm hit with dizziness as the truth slams into me.

"You knew?"

"Of course, I knew. You forget. I covered some of Penn State's games, one in particular—the College World Series against UCLA. I remember one girl who was happy to be in the arms of the winning pitcher."

A blush crosses my face. Oh my God, I can't believe he was there. But that *was* a great night.

"And besides, one look at that adorable girl, and you'd have to be a fool not to know who the father is."

My expression turns cold as I stare him down. When is the line crossed between employee and boss? I work for this man, for crying out loud. He's not my dad.

"So, this is the reason you're pushing me toward him?"

"An opportunity presented itself, and I may have taken advantage," he says, shrugging off my acidic tone.

"What would the *Times* say knowing you spent their money toward personal gain?"

"Please. I couldn't care less what they said. But if it makes you feel better, I picked up most of the tab."

No, that doesn't make me feel better. It makes me feel worse.

"I'll repay you."

"Nonsense. I did it on my own. Now, go get busy. You need to get going to beat rush hour traffic."

Flashes of Zoe's happiness replay through my mind, and my hatred somewhat thaws. Larry had my best interest at heart. I shouldn't be mad at him. The person to be mad at is me.

"Larry, thanks for what you've done. Zach spent time with Zoe on Sunday. I'm not sure that would've happened if you hadn't interfered."

A small smile crosses his face. "I didn't do it all for Zoe. I'm not sure about the details of your breakup. But I do know every time Zach is mentioned a longing crosses your face. Whether you want to admit it or not, you still harbor deep-seated feelings for him. It's up to you to act upon them."

I mumble thanks as he walks away. I pick up the phone and press speed dial number one. It doesn't take long for the female voice to answer.

"Jocelyn, I need another favor."

CHAPTER NINETEEN

ZACH

CURRENT DAY

I TOSS MY LUGGAGE INTO THE TRUNK OF THE CAR AND TURN MY phone back on. I wait for the messages to buzz through. A missed text and call from Lacey has me puzzled. Worried that something happened to Zoe, I open the text first and then pause, rereading her words twice.

Lacey: *Almost to Philly. Can we talk? Officially and unofficially?*

With the foul mood I'm in, I know I won't be up for much conversation. I really wanted to come home and crash. Wallow around in self-pity for an evening. But I can't tell Lacey no. My fingers fly across the screen as I type.

Me: *Of course. I'll be home in two hours.*

I finish typing out my address and slide into the passenger seat. In no time at all, I'm home, and there's a knock on my door.

Before Lacey reentered my life, I'm not going to lie, I've thought about her. A lot. One of the things I've pictured was her sitting on my couch. Of course, there may have been minimal clothing involved and a more relaxed expression upon her face.

This scared, worried look she's sporting never entered my mind. But there she is, her back stiffer than my old wooden bat and concern etched into every facial plane. The problem? I don't know if she's concerned about me, concerned about being here with me, or concerned about what the future holds. Maybe a combination of all three?

One thing's for sure, I hate the idea of the mother of my daughter unable to relax in my home. Wine is in order. We both could use something to take the edge off.

"Here," I say as I hand her the wine glass and sit on the opposite end of the couch. I need to maintain a safe distance away from her. I don't want to risk our legs touching. My mind may be mad as hell at her, but my body is singing her praises. "You don't have to be so uptight around me."

Her gaze sweeps to mine.

"I don't mean to be. I just … I know you hate me right now."

Crap. Lacey's concerned about being here with me.

"Look, I was mad." I grip the stem of my glass tighter. "I still am, but I could never hate you. There's too much history between us."

Her eyes soften as she bites her lower lip. That plump lip that I love to gnaw on. I force myself to look away and take a sip of wine. Those thoughts need to stay at bay. But damn, if I'm not craving another taste.

"You want to know about my shoulder?" I switch to a safer topic.

"My boss asked me to come here for an exclusive, but it's more of a ploy to get us to talk. Much to my surprise, he figured out you were Zoe's father long before that press conference. Ever since an opportunity arose, he's been pushing your story on me. I just figured out the reason why today."

"What all happened back then? How'd you end up working for him?"

"Well, you know he got me that awesome internship. Soon after I started, I found out I was pregnant. There wasn't any way I could pursue that career. I needed a job that paid money because I needed to take care of my baby. So, when they asked me to continue for another six months, I turned them down. Larry caught wind of it and called, asking why I didn't seize the opportunity. I had no choice but to tell him I was pregnant. He still failed to see the problem until I told him I needed a higher paying job. I couldn't work a year for basically peanuts."

I swallow back my "I could've helped" response. We don't need to rehash the past. But I made enough money to support us. I worked hard and dedicated every minute to improving my craft. That reason alone is why the Phillies agreed to my agent's contract but also the reason my major league debut occurred near the end of that first year. Damn, she may have been right in letting me pursue my career. I don't mention that, though.

"What about your parents?" It's a dick question to ask. It's hardly their responsibility, but they haven't appeared at all in this equation. I know they're not poor. They could've helped.

"That's basically what Larry asked after I told him I didn't know who the father was, but no. I didn't have their support. Larry took pity on me and offered me a job in his office. I've been there ever since."

"I don't understand why your parents wouldn't help you out."

Her facial expression falls immediately as she glances at the floor. A pang of sadness rips through to my core. She looks so damn defeated. I naturally gravitate toward her, leaning forward a bit. I rest my left arm behind her on the back of the couch and hide my wince. The sharp pain has me withdrawing my arm fast. Shit, I need to remember not to pivot my shoulder.

"They didn't agree with me not telling you. I tried to explain that you broke up with me so you wouldn't have any distractions. I stressed how important establishing your baseball career was, not only for you but your family. I left the part out about seeing you; they didn't need to know that. But still, they refused to understand, and honestly, their opinion didn't matter. I wasn't going to ruin your shot at making the pros."

My jaw clamps shut as I try my hardest to listen. I don't say I'm sorry. It won't do any good now. It hurts hearing how selfish I was, but I can't change my past behavior. I have to own it, but I understand Lacey's reasoning for not telling me better. A noble, unselfish act on her part but still wrong.

"Even though they disagreed with my reasoning, they respected my choice. Grandpa was the only one who halfway understood, but even he tried to talk me into telling you. So, they basically turned away from me, and I moved to the city to start over."

"You've been pretty much solo since?"

"I've had Jocelyn. Without her, I'm not sure what I would've done."

I stare at her for a moment. The urge to reach across and hold her, protect her, surges through me. I press my balled fists into my thighs to stop myself. It pisses me off that her family turned away from her when she needed them the most. Things would've been so different had she told me. I can't believe she endured so much on her own. Now would be the time my anger should lessen because this sure as hell hasn't been easy for her, but for some reason, I can't let it go. But I don't have to be a dick.

"I'm sorry you went through that by yourself, but from now on, you have me to lean on. I'll always be there for our daughter. That, you can count on."

Tears well in her eyes as she nods in understanding. I switch the subject once again to the current dilemma facing us.

"They did another MRI on my shoulder. The doctor said it's tendinitis." My somber tone doesn't improve our situation, but I accomplish my goal of shifting the focus to my problems instead of hers. Seeing her upset still guts me.

"That's good though, right?"

"Yeah, but I have to rest for a month and then start conditioning in the minors. Hopefully, I'll be back in time before the playoffs."

"Zach, I'm so sorry. I know how badly you want to be with the team."

"Yeah, it sucks. But the trainer's afraid I'll damage the tissue further. There's no tear, though. So, that's good news. I guess we'll see."

She gives me a sympathetic smile.

"In the meantime, I'd like to spend as much time with my daughter as possible. I'll put myself up in a hotel and try not to make you sick of me." I throw her my grin that always got me my way.

Her ringtone interrupts her response. But if the smile she's trying her damnedest to hide is any indication, I think she'll agree. She eyes the screen and presses ignore, but I catch sight of the name Brayden Hicks. Isn't he the prick that pushed his way to her during my press conference? I'm pretty sure that's the same name that was displayed on his badge.

I study her face and relax somewhat when she doesn't seem thrilled. Not that it matters. The last thing I want to do is start a relationship with her. Not while this anger still festers inside. I toss my ill-placed jealousy aside and continue.

"The rehab they want me to do can be done in New York, but I'm pretty sure rest is on the agenda for the next few weeks."

"That sounds great. I know Zoe would want that. But staying in a hotel for a month? Wouldn't that be expensive."

I press my lips together to suppress a smile. Lacey has no idea. I don't want to brag, but I've made enough money through the years to where I can afford a month's stay in a hotel. My gaze falls around my small but decent-sized two-bedroom apartment. I have minimal decor. Couch, recliner, television, I'm good. I've spent my money wisely.

"I'll make do," I say.

The concern grows in her eyes, and I can't tell what she's contemplating. Guilt? Confusion?

"My house is small, or I'd offer you a room."

"Thanks for the offer, but I think things would be a little weird. And I don't want to confuse Zoe."

She nods and glances at the clock on the wall. As she stands, she runs her hands down her skirt, and I can't help but notice her muscular legs. The memory of those legs wrapped around me as I thrust into her the other night jolts through my body. The thrill is short-lived, shut down from the loss of what we could have had.

"Do you need a cab?" I ask.

"No, I drove."

The tension remains strained between us as we walk downstairs and make our way to her car. From our very first date, the conversation flowed easily between us. This new level of uncomfortableness feels odd. Different. I don't like it. The clicking from the car's lock mechanism breaks the silence. I reach around her and open the driver's door.

Mistake. Big one.

As she bends to get inside, my body stiffens when a hint of strawberry wafts through the air. Her lying beneath me with her strawberry-scented hair splayed across my bed fills my vision.

"Lacey," I say, strangulated. She pauses, lifting her face to mine and staring directly at me. My heart races as our lips are mere inches away from each other. Her gaze drops to my mouth, and that's all it takes. I can't fucking breathe; I want to close the gap between us so badly and claim what's supposed to be mine. I grip the doorframe tighter and force myself to speak. "I-I'll call you when I get to town."

She swallows hard and looks away. The glistening in her eyes nearly kills me.

"I'll see you then," she says and then slips inside.

As the taillights fade in the distance, I feel as if my whole world came crashing down and there's not a Goddamn thing I can do about it. The next few weeks will prove interesting. But I'm looking forward to them. Even though it will be rough being close to Lacey without touching her, I still can't wait to know my little girl.

CHAPTER TWENTY

LACEY

CURRENT DAY

Zoe and I barely get inside the house when the front doorbell rings. I cringe from her piercing squeal, but as Zoe tosses her backpack down and jolts to the door, hands clapping, I can't help but smile. She's so excited. Zach told her he was coming during their FaceTime call last night, and she's been talking nonstop about him ever since.

"My daddy's coming to visit me tonight," she said on our way to preschool. "I'm going home so my daddy can visit me," she told Jocelyn's clan before we left for home. In the car on the way here, she kept saying how she couldn't wait to show him her "surprise." I wish I had the same enthusiasm.

After leaving his apartment two nights ago, the realization that he'll never forgive me smacked me right in the face. I know he wants me physically—that's apparent by his body language—but when faced with a decision to act on it, he shies away. I try to convince myself that's what I want—a pure platonic-based friendship so we can be civil around our daughter—but my hormones beg a different story.

The way he conducted himself proves that he hates me more than his desire to kiss me. Argh! I can't even be mad at him. This crushing guilt that occurs every time I think about what I've done doesn't allow me to.

"Hurry up, Mommy," Zoe says, bouncing on her feet.

I snap out of my funk and hurry to the door.

"Daddy," Zoe yells as soon as the door swings open.

"Hey, pumpkin," Zach leans down to her outstretched arms and embraces her. "How was preschool?"

"Fun! I made a picture." She shimmies out of his arms and runs to her backpack lying on the couch. She unzips the top and runs back over with the paper waving in the breeze. "Look, I drew you today."

I bite my lip at the three stick figures—two large ones and a smaller one in between with their hands interlocked. Big bright blue eyes cover the misshaped heads of the taller figure on the left and the small middle figure. Red squiggly lines adorn the figure to the right. I can only interpret that mess as my hair. After studying the picture, I conclude my baby girl will never be considered Picasso, but there's no mistaking the smiles she drew on their faces. She's depicted us as one happy family. Another pang of guilt punches through my chest.

"Aw, look at that. You're a natural. Is that you?" Zach's sexy grin shines as he points to the one in the middle. Zoe nods, her eyes gleaming bright and shiny.

"That's you, and that's Mommy. We're happy because we love each other and we're together."

Zach's gaze shifts to mine, and I'm stunned, rooted in place. This is the first time Zoe's referred to us as a family, but I'm not sure how to digest that information. What is the best way to approach that subject with her?

"I do love you, Zoe." Zach leans in and kisses the top of her head.

"I have a surprise for you." Her face lights up again.

"Another one?" Zach chuckles.

"Yeah, wait here." She turns and her little legs race across the floor toward her room.

"Looks like we have a future artist on our hands." The corners of his mouth twitch.

"Yeah, a starving one." We laugh, and I glance sideways at him, our gazes locking. My laughter fades as every ounce of desire I ever had springs forward. If only he could work through his anger. "I-I better get supper started, or we'll be eating late." I stalk to the kitchen, but Zach's hot on my tail.

"Lacey." He grabs my arm, and his warm touch causes me to halt. "Thanks for letting me come over. I do appreciate it."

I take a deep breath and turn to face him. His eyes bore into mine with a haunted look, or maybe one of regret. My throat thickens. "Zach, I'm—"

"Daddy, look!" Zoe runs back into the room with a grin stretching from ear to ear.

His arm drops as he turns to face Zoe. When he sees her outfit, he throws a quick appreciative glance my way before focusing his attention to his number one fan. "Now you're styling. I love it."

I'm sure he recognizes the Phillies baseball cap he gave me before leaving. I let Zoe have it when I explained which team her daddy plays for. She's been proudly wearing it around the house ever since.

Zoe turns around to display the back of her jersey. "Mommy bought this for me." Her tone grows serious as she adds, "It's your number."

"Why yes, it is." Zach turns to me and mouths a thank you. In one quick motion, he scoops Zoe in his arms. She giggles as he carries her off into the living room. "I can't think of anyone else who would look this great wearing my number."

As I reach for the frying pan, I say a silent thank you to modern technology. If it weren't for FaceTime, Zach would still be a stranger. Talking with each other the past few nights has brought them closer together with each time getting less awkward. Even if their conversation only consists of her telling him about daycare or her afternoon over at Jocelyn's house, the visual of Zach's face, while they talk, makes him real. He's no longer a stranger to her, or her to him.

As I cook, I can't stop the occasional smile every time I hear Zoe squeal from laughter. She's clearly happy. That makes him hating me worth it. In no time at all, supper is finished, and we're sitting around the small kitchen table, eating.

"Have you given any thought as to where you want to live?" Zach asks as he scoops green beans onto his plate.

"Uh, no. Not yet." The truth is, I haven't had time to think about where to move. I half-thought he wasn't serious. Or maybe it was wishful thinking. With working my crazy hours, I can't imagine the stress of looking for a new home.

"Are we moving with you, Daddy?"

"No," I say rushed. My eyes meet Zach's panicked expression, and I suppress a smile. Although I'll admit, it hurts that the mere thought of living with us causes pure panic. "Remember, Daddy lives in another state."

"Yeah, I know."

The sadness in her tone causes another pang of regret to hit my chest, but I must remember no matter if I had told him or not, he'd still be living elsewhere.

"But Trenna lives with her mommy and daddy."

"That's because they're married." I shift my gaze back to Zach. "Trenna is Jocelyn and Carl's daughter."

Zach lowers his fork and turns to face Zoe. "I was hoping to find a bigger house for you in a different area. One with a backyard to play in. Would you like that?"

"I guess so." Zoe's voice grows silent, and my heart squeezes at her disappointment.

Zach looks back at me and asks, "Any ideas on the school districts? I can start looking this week after rehab."

"I-I'm not sure. I haven't really given it much thought," I stammer.

"I'll do some checking around."

I remain quiet, not sure what to think about this. It's not like I'm opposed to Zoe attending good schools, but Zach can't waltz in here and dictate major changes.

Zoe drags out her *Frozen* game after she shoveled the last bite of food into her mouth. The discussion of life-altering moves pauses for now, and I shrug it off. I'm not letting it ruin our time.

The last part of the evening winds down, and soon it's time for Zoe's bedtime rituals. This is the first time Zach can tell her goodnight in person. It's rather surreal watching her hug him so tightly.

"All right, sweetheart. I'll be back tomorrow night."

"You will?" she asks with a mixture of sleepy surprise.

"You bet. Now get some sleep." A pained expression crosses his face as he stares at her. "I love you, Zoe."

Zach's voice cracks at the end, and I suddenly find it hard to breathe. Watching their exchange is bittersweet as guilt flares up again.

"I love you, Daddy." She gives another tight squeeze before letting go. When Zach covers her up with her pink blanket, she murmurs, "I love you, Mommy."

"I love you, too. You better get some shuteye."

Zach joins me by her door, and then we turn and walk down the hallway. The air is so thick I have absolutely no idea how to remedy the situation.

"You don't get to spend much time with her, do you?" Zach asks, breaking the awkward silence.

"No. Not with work, the hour commute, and preparing supper." I head straight to the kitchen to work on the dishes. "It makes for a long day."

Zach frowns but doesn't say anything more. "I'll help you clean up."

"You don't have to."

"It's the least I can do after that great meal." He stretches and rubs his stomach. "It's been awhile since I've had an actual home-cooked dinner."

A smile breaks across my face. His statement shouldn't make me happy, but knowing that my cooking brought him happiness makes me feel good.

We're down to the last dish on the table as we walk to the sink. I open the dishwasher and bend over right as Zach stretches across to place a dish on the counter. My bottom brushes against his pelvis, and oh my God, a multitude of things occurs at the same time. Every nerve ending lights with fire, and I bite my tongue to stop the threatening moan from escaping. Zach's breath hitches as his body stiffens against me. His hands grab hold of my hips and his fingers dig into my flesh. He pulls me closer and nuzzles his chin in the crook of my neck. My heart races as his warm breath tickles my ear and spearmint floods my senses. Then, the sensations disappear as he steps away.

I close my eyes and chastise myself for wanting more. More of his touch. More of his body. But I'm not alone in those thoughts. The ragged, short breaths behind me suggest this is as hard on him as it is on me.

"No matter how much I want you, please understand *nothing* can happen between us."

I swallow down the pain that statement causes and turn toward him, making my face as stoic as possible.

"Of course, I wasn't trying to—"

"I know you weren't. But I want to make it clear that I'm not sure if I'll ever be able to forgive you."

He may as well have stuck a dagger into my heart because the pain searing through my chest can't tell the difference. I'm trying my best to mask the hurt, but I'm not sure if I'm succeeding. I give a curt nod and turn back toward the dishes before the tears I've been suppressing spring forward.

"I'll ... I'll see myself out."

I remain quiet and concentrate on the dishes. When the front door swings shut, I release a long, shaky breath. I don't think I'm strong enough to survive the next few weeks.

CHAPTER TWENTY-ONE

LACEY

CURRENT DAY

NIGHT GAMES ARE THE WORST. AS A FAN OF BASEBALL, THAT statement makes me sad, because those games used to excite me. The anticipation of waiting the entire day. The electric charge of the crowd. The illumination of the park under the floodlights. I loved it all, until now. Now, they mean I don't get to see my daughter. To be fair, Larry's been easy on me so far, scheduling me during the day games, but that's only going to last for so long. Eventually, I'll have to start pulling my weight and cover those cherished prime spots.

But those evening games come with an exchange of missing my daughter.

As I pull into my driveway, I try to ignore the rush of warmth the soft amber lighting emitting through the living room window causes. Zach's been visiting Zoe every night for the past two weeks, but this is the first time I'm coming home late. Knowing Zoe's tucked safely in her bed and Zach sprawled out on my couch —which my mind totally paints a picture of him that way—makes his presence seem normal. Like a family. Like it should be.

But that scene isn't reality. Thinking of us as a family comes with a price of toying with my heartstrings.

Not wanting to risk waking Zoe, I park in the driveway and then gather my purse and briefcase. I quickly exit to the front door ready to be inside. My purse slides down my shoulder as I fumble to find the correct key. I should've remembered to turn the porch light on before leaving. It's way too dark. I jump with a start as the door swings open.

"Thanks. I should've had my key ready." I laugh and toss an appreciative glance toward Zach.

Zach scans behind me, frowns, and then shifts to the side, opening the door wider.

"I hate this neighborhood. Especially at night. It isn't safe for you to be coming home so late."

"I suppose." I downplay his concern and change subjects. "Did Zoe give you any problems?"

I'm reaching. I know darn well she was good for him, but I don't want to discuss moving again. We haven't looked at any houses yet. Zach's been compiling a list of schools he deems appropriate for Zoe, but there's a few more that he wants to check out before home searching. I'll let him do his research, and then I'll pick from his top five. That's all I have time for.

"Not at all. Rehab didn't last that long today, so I picked her up from Jocelyn's early and took her to the park." A pinkish tint creeps on his face as the right side of his mouth draws up. "We may have had ice cream, and I kind of spoiled her a bit. Hope you don't mind."

I suppress my grin. Seeing this big domineering male reduced to a shy little teddy bear is quite comical. But considering he's been hands off the entire two weeks we've been together, and he hasn't made one single move toward me, I'm sure nothing will ever happen between us again.

But it has been nice having him here. I must admit; however, it's exhausting keeping up the cooking routine. Some days I like to cheat but can't do that with him around. I don't want him thinking

I'm a bad mom. And he's been great with Zoe. She loves having him here. It's when she goes to bed that gets weird. There's always a slight awkwardness between us, which I hate.

"My trainer called today."

My stomach flips from his words as I drop my purse and briefcase onto the couch. I've been having bouts of queasiness today anyway, but the sudden seriousness of his tone doesn't settle well.

"What did he say?" I slowly turn to face him.

"They want me to report down in Florida earlier than expected. I leave in another week. I'm sorry. I thought I would have the full four weeks to stay here."

This news shouldn't upset me. I shouldn't care, but I've kind of gotten used to him being around. And admittedly, it's been nice.

"I have an idea. I'm just not sure if you're going to agree to it."

I lift my chin to him as I try to contemplate what on earth he could be talking about.

"Move in with me."

"What?" I shake my head in disbelief. My legs turn to Jell-O, resulting in my sudden plop on the couch. "What do you mean? Like, move to Philly?"

"It's an option." He stands, towering above me as if moving in with him is the answer to everything. His casual expression pisses me off.

"I have to work, Zach."

"I make more than enough for the both of us, and besides, I'm rarely around. I'm sure there are other affiliates that would be happy to hire you."

This is insane, and so out in left field I'm not sure he's thought this through. I think he just wants to be with Zoe.

"Do you love me?"

"Of course, I do. I always have."

That causes me to pause. I half-expected Zach to say no since he's been so angry with me. Two weeks ago, he declared nothing could ever happen between us. Did the realization that he's going to be leaving change his mind?

"And you've forgiven me." I snap my fingers. "Just like that?"

Warning bells alarm from his hesitation, and I curse silently to myself. He almost had me.

"I think you have your answer."

"Give it some thought. I'm not talking about being a couple, but it'd be easier if we lived together."

I hold my tongue. Easier for him, maybe. The ping from my text alert cuts through the silence. I pull the phone out and don't miss Zach's jaw stiffening from the site of Brayden's name.

"He's only texting to check on me," I explain and then wonder why I feel the need for an explanation. How does he even know Brayden anyway? But that brings up a good point. "What would happen when one of us wants to date?"

He inhales sharply as his eyes narrow.

"I have no desire to date anyone else," he says dismissively.

"For now, but what about later? No woman in her right mind would want the baby momma living in with her boyfriend. Did you not learn anything from Rachael and Ross?"

He pins me with a somber expression, clearly unappreciative of *Friends*. "Why are you asking about that? Do you want to date other men?"

"What? No—" My phone's ringtone interrupts the point I wanted to make.

"You better get that."

Zach's angry tone throws me off guard, but I obey and glance at the phone. I feel the blood drain from my face. It isn't Brayden who's calling; it's Jocelyn. I hit the answer button.

"Jocelyn, what's wrong?" I ask.

Zach's head whips toward mine, his anger stripped away.

"Oh my God. Is he okay?" My gaze flashes to Zach's as tears begin to form. I can't believe this is happening.

"No, don't worry. I'll be right there."

CHAPTER TWENTY-TWO

ZACH

CURRENT DAY

THE TEARS WELLING IN LACEY'S WIDENED, FRIGHTENED EYES when she ends the phone call cut me to the core.

"Did something happen to Carl?" I ask.

"H-h-he's been shot. They're doing surgery on him right now." She swipes her purse off the couch and darts to her shoes.

"Shot? How? Where? Why isn't he at home?"

"He works late a lot." She can barely put her shoes on, her hands are shaking so much.

I raise my eyebrows. "It's pretty damn late," I mumble, not sure why I'm stressing on that point, but can't she see how this doesn't sound right. It's a Friday night. Who works this late on a Friday night? I reach for my shoes and slip them on.

"He's a workaholic and sometimes pulls all-nighters. It's not unusual for him to be gone all night." She stands straight and looks at me with her tear-streaked face. "What are you doing?"

"I'm going to drive you."

"You need to stay with Zoe." Her voice raises a few octaves too high.

"I know. Zoe's coming with us. You're way too upset to drive, and besides, it's late. I don't want you going alone."

"I appreciate the gesture, but—"

"Just wait for me." I cut her off and take off toward Zoe's room. There's no time to waste because Lacey's stubborn. If I dawdle too long, she'll leave without me.

"Hey, baby girl. We're going for a ride."

Zoe stirs but doesn't fully wake. I cradle her in my arms and head back to the door. Anxiety is written all over Lacey's face when I emerge from the hallway.

"I can drive," Lacey says, opening the door for me.

"You're upset. I'll drive."

"Fine."

The fight has left her voice as she hands over the keys, and I ignore her sigh of relief on the way to the car.

Before long, we pull up to the newly constructed, two-story townhome. The neighborhood—seemingly nicer than Lacey's—looks as if it's been renovated within the last five years. When I picked Zoe up the other day, I thought about an area like this for them to live. But I'd rather have them live with me. That's the better choice.

Lacey goes on ahead of me as I tend to Zoe. Jocelyn's grief-filled shriek carries through the air, and at my approach, she breaks away from Lacey's hug. She turns to me with a small attempt at a smile. Her blotchy red face makes me squeamish. I hate when females cry. Since the age of ten, I grew up with a houseful of men, so I'm not adapted to deal with feelings and shit.

"Hey, Jocelyn. I'm so sorry," I say for lack of better words.

"Zach, it's good to see you." Her voice breaks as she crosses her arm to hang onto a quaking shoulder. "Follow me. You can put Zoe in my bed."

I follow her down the dimly lit hallway and place Zoe under the comforter. Her eyes open for a second before she rolls to her side.

"Go back to sleep, sweetheart," I whisper.

"'Kay, Daddy."

Jocelyn lets out a whimper and retreats to the door. I take a few long strides to catch up to her.

"Hey, hopefully, he'll be okay," I say. Jocelyn nods but looks so defeated I'm not sure whether to embrace her or not. We step back toward the living room with me asking, "Did you need me to drive you to the hospital?"

"My brother-in-law will be here soon to pick me up. Thanks, though."

When we rejoin Lacey, Jocelyn informs us the details behind Carl's shooting. She thinks he must've left something in his car since he was shot on a sidewalk. She insists they mugged him on his way to the parking garage. To me, the story doesn't jive, but I don't voice my opinion out loud. I really don't know Carl, other than the fact that Jax loathed him. When Lacey and I dated, we never hung around them enough for me to formulate an opinion about him.

Headlights shine through the window prompting Jocelyn to shuffle to the door.

"I'm not sure what time I'll be back in the morning." Jocelyn turns to me and says, "I'm glad you're here for Lacey, Zach."

"Take as long as you need. I've got the kids covered," Lacey pipes up. "Plus, I don't have to work tomorrow since I worked late tonight. Ben's covering the afternoon game."

I look at Lacey and smile. She's such a sacrificing person. Self-less to the core. A rare trait, especially in the circle of people I've dealt with.

"Thank you." Jocelyn's voice cracks again as she slips through the door's entrance.

"He better be okay." Lacey plops on the couch rubbing her temples. "It's not fair."

I sit beside her and draw her into my chest. The strawberry scent of her hair invades my senses, but I squash that feeling. All Lacey needs from me is a shoulder to cry on.

"He's one of the good guys, you know. They built this incredible life together. They may have been forced into marriage, but they've been perfect."

"Forced?" What the hell did she mean by that? This isn't the medieval times.

"Jocelyn got pregnant about two months after I found out about Zoe. Carl was set to propose anyway, but when the sonogram showed twins, they eloped. Tristan and Trenna are four, and Melanie is one."

My back stiffens but Lacey's so upset, I doubt she notices. I'm instantly jealous of Carl's family life.

It doesn't take long before Lacey falls asleep. Carefully inching out from underneath her, I lay her down on the couch and slip a pillow under her head. I grab the blanket and drape it across her. Lacey stirs, lips parting. She looks so angelic and peaceful. I'm hit by a pang of yearning. I reach out, wanting a piece of her silky, soft skin, but I stop myself. Instead, I study her rhythmic breathing. But pictures of something awful happening to her invade my thoughts. Anything from a mugging to a simple car wreck could happen. My chest fills with anxiety. I can't think about that. If something bad were to happen, I'd be devastated.

Maybe I've been too much of a jughead. Hell, I saw what happened on the field when I couldn't focus. Would I have become the pitcher that I am today with those distractions back then? Was she right? I'll gladly trade the last five years to have been with my baby girl, but fuck if I know how I would've supported them. Baseball is all I've ever done. The only thing I'm good at.

I blow out a breath as I stare at her. I was serious earlier about having her live with me, and I think it could work. No, I *know* it could work. When we find out Carl's outcome, I'll bring this up. I step away from the couch and settle into the recliner. Will she be able to forgive me, though? And not just for my recent behavior but for my past indiscretion. We were broken up, but she's right. It was only three months after our breakup. I wouldn't have handled seeing her leaving a guy's room. Fuck. I couldn't handle seeing Brayden's name on her phone. Yeah, I can see how she would be hurt. Now, I need to figure out how to win her back.

✄

THE SLAM OF THE FRONT DOOR JARS ME AWAKE. I RELEASE THE recliner mechanism and sit upright, turning to look at Jocelyn storming through the door. *Oh boy.* What was a distraught frail girl last night has morphed into one pissed-off woman. I'm afraid my assumptions were right. Jocelyn's seething.

"What's the problem?" Lacey asks, raising into a sitting position. "How's Carl?"

"Still alive, but he won't be after he wakes."

"What are you talking about?"

Jocelyn stalks over to the couch and sinks into the cushions. She places her elbows on her thighs and covers her face with her hands.

"I'm so humiliated," she murmurs.

"You're not making sense."

Jocelyn's hands slide down her face as she glances at Lacey. "Carl's been cheating on me."

Lacey rears back as shock covers her features, and those jealous feelings I had of Carl's perfect life disappear. Stupid prick. I'm by far not perfect, but one thing I don't condone is cheating. I'm with Jax on that one.

"I'm totally blindsided by this. How can Carl have done this to me?"

The term third wheel comes to mind, and I feel as if I'm intruding. "I'll go make us some coffee."

I stand, and Lacey tosses a sympathetic look my way and then scoots closer to Jocelyn, wrapping an arm around her shoulders.

"The late-night work sessions," Lacey says knowingly.

"God, how could I have been so stupid?" She leans her head on Lacey's shoulder.

"H-how did you find out?"

153

KIMBERLY READNOUR

I'm working around her kitchen, looking for the coffee container and trying not to eavesdrop, but their voices carry.

Apparently, a fight had broken out not too far from the entrance of some club. When Carl and his date stepped outside, a gun was fired, and the stray bullet found Carl's abdomen. Luckily for him, it missed his vital organs. Although he may wish it hadn't after Jocelyn gets through with him.

I bring in their coffee at the tail end of their conversation.

"Too bad the bullet didn't hit him in his balls," Jocelyn says in a flat tone.

I hold back my choke. Jesus, remind me not to piss Jocelyn off. The sound of pattering feet hushes Jocelyn, and the ladies move into the kitchen.

Lacey shoots me a sad smile, but she's not making eye contact. I can't imagine what's going through her mind. She was just saying how Carl was such a great guy. Is not was. He's not dead, just no longer "great."

"Who are you?" A small, dark-haired boy asks.

"That's my daddy," my little pixie yells as she runs and squeezes my leg tightly.

Both women look at me, and their sad, hardened expressions turn sappy. Lacey's gaze connects with mine, and that point I just know. We belong together. I can no longer deny my feelings. Life's too short to let anger dictate your life choices. Besides, my anger subsided earlier. As I stare back at her green-speckled eyes, the map to our future carves a path in my mind as if it's been there the entire time. There's one part left to do, and that is to convince my woman she belongs to me.

CHAPTER TWENTY-THREE

LACEY

CURRENT DAY

ZOE BOUNCES ON HER TOES AS ZACH PLACES THE BLUE TUNIC over her. Her constant movement is making it difficult for him to tie it up. I believe the water-based paint will come out if she accidentally drops some on her clothes, so it's not a big deal if it's loose. I suppress a laugh. The mural wall at the Children's Museum of Manhattan has met its match with Zoe.

With a shaky start to the day, Zach's idea to visit the upper east side is just what we needed. I hated to leave Jocelyn today, but she's going to spend the day at the hospital. Maybe I should've volunteered to go with her, but she insisted I spend the day off with Zoe. She claims because of my lack of time with her, but I know there's an ulterior motive behind her actions.

When Zach suggested taking us girls out, I jumped at the chance. Other than spending the evenings at my house, we haven't done anything exciting. And I live in New York City, for crying out loud.

Zoe plants a huge smile on her face as she hops over to the mural. She loves to mix colors and finger paint.

"She seems rather excited," Zach says as he waltzes over and stands beside me.

"Yep, finger painting is one of her favorite things to do." I glance up at him as he watches Zoe. His eyes hold a certain level of appreciation, but it's his overall stance that has me confused. He seems more relaxed today than he has the past couple weeks.

His sideways glance holds me captive as flutters overtake my stomach. There's definitely something different about him today. The longer he stares, heat flares in his eyes. My throat tightens, and I can hardly swallow.

"I was serious about you coming to live with me." He turns his body to face me.

My mouth opens, but nothing comes out. Live with him? He can't be serious. How would it work? Carl comes to mind. The perfect world my best friend lived in was shattered in a matter of a phone call. Nothing is perfect. Our relationship has been far from perfect.

I take a calming breath to try to think clearly. "Do you think you could forgive me? Are you ready to forgive me?"

"I think the bigger question is can you forgive me?"

My face crumbles as a strangulated moan flees from my chest. "I already have."

"I'm totally serious. Move in with me."

"What? As friends?"

"As a couple. I fucking love you, Lacey."

"What about my job?"

"Do you want to keep working?"

I bite my lip. I'm not sure giving up my livelihood to follow a boy would be the wisest decision, but Zach's far from "just some boy." He's the only man I ever loved. And he just confessed his love for me. Why not give us a chance? Give the family a chance?

"Not really." Crappity, crap, crap. I'm totally considering this.

A smile breaks across Zach's gorgeous features, and I can feel my will slowly dissolve.

"I-I don't know. I'm so confused."

"That's not a no." He bends down and wraps his arms around my waist. "You don't have to answer right away. I'll give you a few hours."

I swat his chest and glance upward. The teasing gleam in his eyes tugs my heart. It'd be so easy to push every worry aside and agree. But so much is at stake. So much to consider.

"Mommy, Mommy, Mommy," Zoe says, running toward us, her blue eyes bright and shiny. "Look, Daddy, looky at what I made."

Zach kneels on one knee and side hugs Zoe while commenting on the rainbow of swirls covering the paper.

It doesn't matter what her painting looks like. If someone displayed this scene—Zach's arm draped around Zoe with her widened eyes full of excitement as she points to the paper and me standing right next to them, weaving my fingers through his hair—it'd be the best-framed picture in the entire museum.

There are many things to consider with moving: Jocelyn's new mess she must deal with, my career path, and Zoe. Well, if it were strictly about Zoe, there wouldn't be any hesitation.

Zach peers up at me as if I'm the only person who matters. From that look alone, I'd move in a heartbeat. But I can't make a rash decision. Zach may have been joking about the few hour time frame, but he's impatient and doesn't have long before reporting down to Florida for his rehab stint. He'll be expecting an answer tomorrow, and there are many things to consider.

CHAPTER TWENTY-FOUR

LACEY

CURRENT DAY

"What do you mean you're contemplating moving in with Zach?"

I hold the phone away from my ear as Jocelyn's voice goes from pleasant to shrill.

"What's there to think about?" she continues.

"You wouldn't think it's crazy to quit my job and traipse across the country to live with a guy I barely know?"

"It's only a couple hours' drive, not clear across the country. Besides, you and Zach have always had a special bond. I saw the way he eyed you this morning. He's every bit in love with you as he was in college. It doesn't matter the time span. Not when it comes to true love."

True love. The thing is, no matter how hard I convinced myself I hated that guy, I never truly did. Every time I looked at Zoe, it was a constant reminder of him. I know he wants to be with Zoe, but I'm afraid his sudden forgiveness for me may be a knee-jerk reaction to Carl's near-death experience.

"I'd feel awful leaving you."

"Babe, you have to do what's best for you and Zoe. I told you your day would come. Take advantage of it."

"Yeah, but the timing is off. I won't be around to help you through this rough patch—"

"Rough patch? I'm freaking getting a divorce. The Asshole's awake and all apologetic, but this affair came out of nowhere for me. Despite the fact he's been with her for two years. Two years!"

Clearly, she's done discussing my move. I settle on the couch and snuggle with a blanket as she vents her anger.

Zach left after Zoe crashed from the spectacular day we had together. I came so close to asking him to spend the night, but I think we better approach that cautiously. It's been five weeks since we had our all-night sexcapade. And even though the toe-curling kiss he left me with still sends tingles through my body, it's his whispering for me to think over his proposal that has me warm and tingly inside.

"I'm so sorry, Jocelyn. Carl clearly didn't see what he had in front of him."

"What I don't understand is why he insisted on having another child? Because during my entire pregnancy with Melanie, he was with her."

I'm not sure how to answer that. I don't know why anybody would bring a child into a marriage when they're not fully committed. My eyes grow wide, and my mouth dries. As Jocelyn keeps talking, my mind starts to calculate the days since my last period. When I figure out that I'm two weeks late, my heart starts to flutter. Oh no, not again. I don't mention anything to Jocelyn. She has enough on her plate. But shit. What if I'm pregnant? Maybe it's my nerves. Yeah, I've heard stress could delay menstruation, and it's not like I've never been late before. I'll wait until Zach has gone to Florida before panicking.

"But enough about my situation, when are you moving?"

"What? I'm not sure I am. I still have to decide. Besides, I have work to think about."

"Please, you've been complaining about the job taking time

away from Zoe anyway. You'll find something in Philadelphia if you want to work. But personally, I think some time off is way overdue. When was the last time you took a vacation?"

"Never."

"Exactly! You've worked your butt off from the first day you found out you were pregnant. If anyone deserves a break, it's you."

"I have to talk it over with my boss."

"No, you don't. You just call him and say I'm done."

"I may need his reference." I laugh.

"Fine. Let me know when you talk to him."

"Will do."

We hang up, and I rub my face in frustration. Walking away from Larry is the last thing I want to do right now. I pick up the phone and dial his personal number.

"Lacey, what's up?"

"I need to meet with you, and I don't think it can wait until Monday."

"All right. Where do you want to meet?"

"Jo's. The small diner on the corner of Welsh and Maple."

"I know the place. I'll meet you there tomorrow at nine."

I fire off a text to Zach.

Me: *Can you be here tomorrow at seven. Meeting boss.*
Zach: *I'll be there. You won't regret this.*
Me: *I haven't decided anything.*
Zach: *YET! You forgot the yet.*

I laugh. Same confident Zach. But he's right. I'll decide tomorrow.

CHAPTER TWENTY-FIVE

ZACH

CURRENT DAY

As I sit in the recliner waiting for Zoe to wake, my leg bounces like a jackhammer on speed. I glance at the clock for the twentieth time and groan. Can the time move any slower? Shit, I'm anxious. I'm half-tempted to wake up Zoe so I'll have a distraction.

I drop my forehead into my hands and mentally tell myself to calm the fuck down. The dingy, worn carpet grabs my attention. As I study the matted fibers, guilt about our different living arrangements begins to creep its way inside. Straight from college, my agent set me up with a generous contract, and even though I send money to my parents, I still have enough money to support my elaborate living conditions. My apartment isn't fancy. If anything, it's on the conservative side, but it's at least modern. Not this ... this whole "God only knows who's lived here before" seventies vibe. The olive-green carpet and yellow Formica countertops scream "Update me. Please." My two girls have been subjected to these living conditions while I've been pampered. *Fuck.* I'm such an ass. Besides taking care of my parents, I haven't once thought about money. It's apparent Lacey has struggled for the past five years.

That's going to change.

Standing abruptly, I whip out my phone and dial Jax's number. The team is playing on the West Coast again, but I don't give a flying fuck how early it is. I need to talk to someone. This waiting for Lacey to get back is killing me.

"What's up?" A groggy voice greets me.

"I asked Lacey to move in with me."

I'm greeted with silence.

"You there?" I glance at the phone to see if the call dropped.

"Yeah, give me a minute."

I hear some ruffling of covers and him mumbling to someone. No doubt, a girl he's shacked up with.

"Okay, I'm back. Now say what?"

"I asked Lacey to move in with me." The path I'm making behind her couch will wear the already worn carpet down to the bare threads, but I can't sit still.

"And you're calling because she said no?"

"Way to believe in me, dickhead. No, she hasn't made up her mind. She's talking to her boss now. I'm at her house, waiting for her to come back. Hopefully, with an answer."

"Jesus, are you sure you're ready for that? An instant family, I mean."

Damn, he's a dick in the morning. But even though he's pissing me off, his question makes me pause. Am I ready? I'm pretty sure I am. The decision may have been made in haste, but it's the correct one. Have I given it much thought? No. But does it feel right? Yes.

"I want my family. I love her, Jax. I always have. You know that."

He sighs. "What you're asking Lacey to do is major, dude. You're basically taking away her job ... her sole source of income. I want you to be a hundred percent sure this is what you want before you disrupt their lives."

I realize what she stands to lose if our relationship takes a dive, but that's not going to happen. Lacey and Zoe are mine now. I'll take care of them. Forever.

"What about your shoulder?"

"It's getting better," I lie.

"Your contract expires at the end of this year. Make sure you discuss the possibility of moving."

"We're a family. It'll be fine." That is, as soon as she agrees to move in with me. But there's no doubt in my mind she will. She has to. No matter what decision she's worked in her head, they're coming home with me. She and Zoe belong with me and nowhere else. I'm not losing them again.

"Well then, congratulations, buddy." Jax's tone brightens. "You're officially a grown up."

The sound of feet pattering down the hallway stops the expletive I was going to call him.

"Uh, I've got to go."

"Same. I've gotta find a way to get this girl to leave."

"Jesus, Jax." I shake my head. That guy will never learn.

"Hey, unlike you, I'm definitely available and very willing." He laughs at my groan. "Kidding aside, I am happy for you. You know I've always liked Lacey."

"Thanks, man. Appreciate it."

"Daddy!" Zoe races over and throws her arms around my legs.

Jax chuckles. "Have fun, man."

I end the call and pick up my girl.

"Where's Mommy?"

"She'll be home in a little while. Let's say I make you some pancakes."

"I want Mickey Mouse ones."

"You do?"

"Yeah, and Mommy puts eyeballs on them."

I don't even try to hold back my smile.

"All right then. Let's go make those Mickey Mouse pancakes with eyeballs." What the hell does she use for eyeballs? Fuck it. I'll wing it. It'll keep me occupied while I wait for Lacey.

ⵊ

Z OE COMES RUNNING BACK INTO THE LIVING ROOM WEARING A pink princess dress. She told me which character she was supposed to be, but I fail at any Disney quizzes. I'll have to buy the entire DVD collection and start watching them.

"Daddy, your crown fell off." Zoe's bottom lip protrudes out. Her tone, a mixture of shock and sadness, brings forth the guilt from taking it off.

"How'd that happen?" I pick up the cardboard foil-covered crown off the floor and pretend to study how such an injustice could occur. "Maybe my head is too big."

"Like your hands?" She giggles.

"Oh, you think I have large hands?" I pretend I'm going to tickle her.

"No!" she screams between laughs. "Use this. All princes wear crowns."

Her hand opens, revealing a pink hairclip. I chuckle as I secure the crown in place. Where on earth did she magically pull this clip from? The things I do for the two girls I love. If any of my team-mates saw me, they'd have enough material to blackmail me for months. I smile down at her. Nobody could rock this look better than me.

"Better?" I ask.

The clicking sound draws our attention to the side door, and Zoe's eyes widen as she runs toward the room.

"Mommy," she yells.

"Hey, squirt." Lacey hugs her daughter and glances at me. The appreciation in her eyes morphs into amusement as she bursts out laughing.

"Is this any way to greet your king?" I upgrade my status as I think of the proper punishment to dole out.

With everything that has happened since that night back in my hotel, I haven't touched Lacey. Not in a sexual way. That will change once we're in my apartment.

"Sorry, Your Majesty," she teases while curtsying. "But I come bearing news."

My heart pounds against my chest awaiting the verdict. I raise my hand to undo the hair clip and remove my crown. I don't want to look ridiculous when the woman I love tells me the best news of my life.

"Yeah?" I ask, trying to sound indifferent. Not sure I pulled it off.

"Zoe," Lacey says, "can you go to your room and put all your favorite toys into a pile."

Confusion crosses Zoe's little features, but she nods. "Okay."

A beat of silence passes as Zoe rushes to her room. I continue to stare at Lacey while she bites her bottom lip. It's obvious she wants us to be alone, but her silence is beginning to wear me down. I take short, shallow breaths in anticipation of her answer. I need to find what happened to my balls. They seem to be missing in action since this woman has brought me to my knees.

"I take it you've come up with a decision?" I step to within a breath's distance between us. Her breathing changes to match mine. I'm not sure what I expected—her waltzing inside happily agreeing—but this unsureness wasn't it. Her not coming home with me isn't an option.

"I had a long talk with Larry, and he brought things to my attention I haven't thought of."

My jaw ticks and the thought of pummeling Larry crosses my mind. *What the fuck? I thought he was Team Zach.*

"Anyway, he pointed out the fact that I'm not truly happy with the work I'm currently doing. I'm good at my job, don't get me wrong, but it wasn't exactly my dream job."

My apologies to Larry.

"He also noted how much I'm in love with you."

Her eyes gloss over, and my chest squeezes so fucking tight, I can hardly breathe. Jesus, I love this girl.

"I love you, too. You know that, right."

She nods and smiles softly. "I want to give us a try."

"Does this mean you're going to live with me and you're willing to transfer to any town I get traded to or sign a new contract with?" I shouldn't ask, but I want clarification. There's no room for miscommunication. Jax is right. I don't have the typical nine-to-five job.

"Yes, Zach. I want to move in with you. And I'm willing to live anywhere you're sent to."

Picking her off the ground, I lean my mouth against her ear and murmur, "From the moment I saw you standing on the base-ball field wearing those black jeggings, you've always been the woman for me. I love you so much. You're not going to regret this."

She smiles widely at me when I replace her back on the floor. One thing for sure, I can't wait to get her in my house. Then she'll be all mine. They both will. Tomorrow. We'll move tomorrow.

CHAPTER TWENTY-SIX

LACEY

CURRENT DAY

THIS IS CRAZY. NUTS. I MUST BE CERTIFIABLY INSANE. WHY THE heck am I so calm? When we left this morning for Zach's apartment, my stomach rolled, but one look at his warm eyes, and calmness trumped all anxiety. I quit my job and moved to a new state to be with this man. I should be nervous as hell, but I'm not.

I shake my thoughts away and kiss Zoe on the cheek. She doesn't stir. I pause and stare at her peaceful expression. Her mouth slightly open. Little puffy cheeks. She's such a blessing. My mother had called her a mistake when I found out I was pregnant. How could she have said that? This perfect angel is no mistake.

My hand automatically splays across my abdomen. And if I'm carrying another gift from God, he or she will never be called a mistake. The suspense is killing me, but I haven't said one word to Zach. I don't plan to either. I'll take the test after he leaves for the last stint of his rehab. He needs to concentrate on returning to play and then on the playoffs. One would think I'd learned my lesson, but it seems there's never a good time to tell him.

I pick up the last empty cardboard box from her room and set it beside Zoe's door. I turn for one last peek at her innocent slumber. Such a switch from the adrenaline rush of earlier today. A smile crosses my lips at the thought of Zoe being so excited about moving here. She couldn't wait to live with her daddy or to see her new bedroom. Funny how fickle kids are. When Zach unlocked the front door, she bolted by us, running straight inside.

"Where's my room?" she asked, hardly able to stand still.

Zach chuckled and then led her over to the stairs. When she approached the top of the landing, she froze in her tracks.

"This is my room?" she asked with her hands clenched into tiny fists and positioned on her hips. She eyed the room as if it was the passage into the *Twilight Zone*.

I couldn't stop my laugh. After reassurances that her room would be restored to the pink princess room of before, she loosened up.

"She seems to be okay, now," Zach says, sliding his arms around me from behind. His warm breath tickles my skin as he wisps my hair to the side and plants his lips on my exposed flesh.

"She'll be fine once she gets used to everything. She's so excited to be here with you."

His hands glide along my hips as his lips continue to softly slide along my neck.

"I hate leaving you guys right now. If I had a choice, I'd rehab in Philly."

"I know. But it's part of the game." I turn to face him. "We'll be fine."

His hands dip along my bottom, down my thighs. My inner muscles clench as heat rises through me. It's been five weeks since we made love. Zach hasn't touched me since the hotel room, but that's going to change rather soon, I think.

He grabs hold of my hand and intertwines our fingers. With a gentle tug, he motions toward the living room. "Come on, I have a surprise for you."

I raise an eyebrow as I study him. His mischievous gleam makes me question what he's done, but I follow him down the stairs. My jaw drops when we enter the living room. Soft jazz plays through speakers while candlelight flickers in the background. I press my lips together and stave off the threatening tears when I notice the plate of cheese and crackers, strategically placed next to the Happy Valley Red wine bottle and glasses.

He went to so much effort.

"Since I can't recreate our first date"—he shrugs—"I thought I'd do the next best thing."

"You won me over that night." I glance up at him. I want to see his face when I confess part of my soul. "I tried to resist you because I thought you were the typical jock. But that date proved there was more to you than partying and girls."

His confident smirk appears as he pulls me into a tight embrace.

"I was never a big partier, but as far as other girls, I just hadn't found the right one. Not until you."

I think I just died a little bit. So much time has passed with both of us longing for each other.

"We've wasted a lot of time, haven't we?"

"Due to my stupidity for letting you go, but that's in the past. We both made mistakes. I'm ready to move past that."

He drags me over to the couch and pours me a glass of wine. After both glasses are filled, he hands me mine and positions himself for a toast.

"To our future." He tips his glass toward mine.

I smile and pretend to sip the wine. Overreaction? Maybe, but one can never be too sure.

The fact that I haven't drunk my wine doesn't seem to register with Zach as he takes my glass and places it on the table next to his. Running the tips of his fingers along the side of my face, he murmurs, "I've wanted to do this all day."

"Do what?" I barely choke out.

He doesn't answer. Instead, he draws me toward him and presses his lips to mine. My body ignites with want. I can't get enough of him. His lips. His mouth. His tongue. I want it all.

My heart thrashes against my rib cage as I weave my fingers into his hair. He pushes me backward to the cushions, tongues still locked. He shifts his weight, so he's barely on top, as he settles between my thighs.

Breaking his mouth away, he then closes his eyes, panting. "You taste so good." His eyes reopen and lock with mine. "Just like my favorite wine."

His hands skim along my sides, working their way to my breasts. With a gentle squeeze, his thumbs graze across my nipples, which harden beneath his touch. He drops his head and nibbles the bud pressing against my thin shirt. The sensations are overpowering, and I don't think I can wait much longer. I'd rip his clothes off right here if the threat of our daughter walking down the stairs didn't exist.

"Zach." His name falls from my mouth in a half-grunt, half-moan.

"Mmm, tell me what you need."

"I need you inside me."

The brilliant sapphires flash to a stormy blue as he releases a guttural moan. "Babe, I'm going to do more than just be inside you."

In a flash, I'm scooped up off the couch and being carried down the hallway.

"Your shoulder," I gasp.

"I'm fine."

I don't worry anymore as we find his bed and christen our first night of living together the right way.

CHAPTER TWENTY-SEVEN

LACEY

CURRENT DAY

THE WATER BEADS SHEETING OFF THE GLASS MAKE IT DIFFICULT to see anything but the tip of the yellow umbrella. As it skips across the sidewalk and disappears, I turn from the window and press my lips into a slanted frown. How can I break the news to these big blue eyes staring at me with anticipation?

"Sorry, sweetie. Going to the park isn't happening anytime soon. We'll have to FaceTime Daddy from home."

Her bottom lip puffs out, and I swear my heart shrinks. Zoe's been talking about FaceTiming her daddy at the swings for the past two days. This summer storm dampens all hope of that happening.

"We'll ask Daddy if he can do it tomorrow. Okay?"

Zoe nods her head. "Okay."

I bite my lip as she moseys back to the couch and slouches into the cushions. Her eyes gloss over as she switches her focus to the television. She so wanted to have her daddy see her on the swings. It's been a week since Zach left, and he's not due to come home for another three. Zoe misses him more than I ever imagined she would. But she's not alone in her misery.

The buzz from my phone snaps me from my thoughts. I glance at the screen and grin. Jocelyn. It's been a few days since we last talked, and I have some news to share with her.

"Guess what?" I ask.

"You know I hate suspense. What's up."

"The rabbit lived."

My plan of going to the pharmacy after Zach left for his rehab was thwarted by Zoe's constant presence. It's probably crazy on my part, but I couldn't make myself buy a pregnancy test in front of her. It just felt wrong. And since moving to a new city means not knowing anyone, Zoe's constantly with me. The test became null and void a few days ago, anyway.

"Shit! Sorry, I'm a horrible friend. I forgot to ask. My life is so crazy right now."

"No worries. I completely understand."

"So, not pregnant. That's good, right?"

"Yeah." It should be a good thing, but happy isn't the adjective I'd use to describe my feelings when Aunt Flo decided to pay a visit. When the cramping began, I was taken aback by the sudden onset of disappointment. "It would've complicated things."

"You don't sound very convincing."

"I don't know. We do need to take our relationship slow. It's for the best."

"Did Zach ever ask if you got pregnant? Or even notice the lack of menstruation when he was around?"

"No."

"What an asshole! Sorry, I know you love him, but really. How can he be so stupid?"

I laugh, nervously.

"To be fair, he has had a lot on his mind. Between finding out about Zoe, us moving in with him, and his looming shoulder problem, his plate's full."

"I suppose." She draws out into a long sigh. "When does he come back home?"

"In a few weeks. They have a seven-day home stand, then they hit the road for ten days." The baseball season will be winding down in a couple of months. Sooner if the team doesn't make the playoffs, but with a five-game lead, their chances are looking good.

"I bet Zoe's ready to be with him again."

I glance over at her. She's attuned to the television, sitting with her legs crossed, foot wagging. "Yeah, she's going to talk to Zach in an hour. She can hardly wait."

"Ah, I'm so happy for her."

"Enough about us. What's going on with you and the kids?"

"They're doing all right. They've gotten adjusted to Carl being gone, but they don't fully understand."

She proceeds to tell me the progress of their divorce. I still have a hard time believing Carl cheated on her. He seemed like a perfect husband. Appearances aren't always as they seem, but man, he fooled us all. After she spills everything there is to talk about, we hang up. I miss my friend but knowing she's a call away or a couple hours' distance helps lessen the sting from not being with her.

The phone buzzes again, and I smile. This call will make a little girl very happy.

"Zoe."

She whips her head toward me.

"It's Daddy time."

CHAPTER TWENTY-EIGHT

ZACH

CURRENT DAY

I SET THE SUITCASES DOWN OUTSIDE THE APARTMENT DOOR AND dig for my keys. It's a practiced maneuver I've done multiple times. The plain metal door greets me with a sense of relaxation. A familiarity of home that lies behind the entryway. Today is no exception. Although, there is the element of surprise. I'm coming home a day early and can't wait to see my girls. *My girls*. Who would have thought? This time apart proved one thing, I don't ever want to be away from them again.

When I left Lacey back in college, I was miserable for several weeks. But it was for the best. Or so I thought at that time. I had a promising career that forced me to focus. That drive kept me from going insane. Now? Even the determination to rejoin the team before the season ends isn't enough to pacify me. I fucking miss my family.

I swing the door open and yell, "Where are my two favorite girls?"

"Daddy." Zoe's shrill voice fills the space. Little sounds of pounding feet come barreling toward me. I bend to one knee and prepare for the impact.

"Zach?" Lacey comes rushing toward Zoe and me. "What are you doing home so soon?"

"They cleared me. I'm to report back to the team, tomorrow. As soon as they told me, I booked the earliest flight I could."

Her arms wrap around me; my nose nestles in her hair. The familiar strawberry scent relaxes me further. I'm home.

The evening winds down, and Lacey bends over to kiss a very passed-out Zoe. A sense of pride swells in my chest from being the luckiest man alive. I grab hold of Lacey's hand and lead her downstairs. There are a few things to discuss, but talking is the furthest thing from my mind. Not after picturing Lacey's curves wrapped around me every time I went to bed these past few weeks. Her memory kept me company during those long-ass evenings. My poor fist has never been through such a workout.

"I talked with McFay. They're placing me in the bullpen," I say reluctantly when we settle on the couch. This won't be a short conversation, but I need to bring it up regardless.

Her eyes flood with concern. "Are you okay with that?"

"Yeah, I think I am. It will be less stress on my shoulder. Lower pitch counts. I feel good, but I want to do what's best for the team and me. I'm back. That is what's important."

"You'll do well in that part of the rotation."

I grab her hand and pull her against me. God, I've missed touching her soft skin. Three weeks is too long to stay away. "You know what else is important? Us."

"Yeah?"

"Yeah." I plant my hand on the nape of her neck and press my lips to hers. Her mouth parts all too eagerly as I thrust my tongue inside, tasting that sweet flavor I've craved.

I lift off the couch, cradling her body against mine, and carry her to our bedroom. There are still a few details left to discuss, but I can't wait any longer. I need to be inside her.

With minimal effort, I lay her on the mattress. My fingers

fumble with the bra clasp as if it's my first time rounding second base. I slip her top off and guide her backward, running my hands along her sides. She's soft and beautiful. My dick throbs with want as I stare at the curves displayed in front of me. I practically rip her pants off and shed my own clothes. Her slow seductive smile makes me about come standing there. What the hell is wrong with me? I'm as excited as the first night when I slammed into her against the brick walls in the dingy alleyway. Kneeling on the mattress between her legs, I reach across and grab the condom from the side table. Once back in position, I pause, my fingers clutching the wrapper. That first night...

"What's the problem?"

My gaze meets hers. "I-I never followed up after our first night together."

"What?" Confusion floods those green hues staring back at me.

My mouth opens, but I can't speak. How could I have been so selfish? *Again?* That night I was careless, but I vowed to follow up. I never did. But she must not be pregnant. I mean, she hasn't said a word about it. But then again, Zoe's proof of how well Lacey can keep a secret. Jesus, I'm so stupid.

"You're on the pill, aren't you?" I blurt without thinking.

She sits up, her mouth agape. I immediately regret my words.

"You're asking me this *now?*"

"Are you?"

"No. I've never been on the pill."

Fuck me.

"So, the night we ... when I—"

Lacey leans forward and places her hand on top of my forearm. I stare at her delicate, elongated fingers and the silky smoothness of her skin. I drag my gaze along the length of her arm, across her perfect tits, and up to those cute freckles splayed across her nose. My eyes inch upward until I meet a softened gaze filled with nothing but concern.

"I'm not pregnant. If that's what you're worried about."

"No, I'm not worried, It's just..." I let my words trail off. *"I'm not pregnant.*" Aren't those the words that every man wants to hear? What I wanted to hear? Shouldn't I be happy or filled with instant relief instead of this...weird sensation of emptiness? I blink away my thoughts. I have this beautiful, willing woman in my bed, and instead of taking advantage of her, I'm acting all emotional and shit. My gaze drops to her naked body that's begging for my touch. I let out a low moan and grip her hips. "Maybe I just need to work on my delivery."

Lacey yelps as she falls back into the bed, and I flip her over to her stomach.

"Get on all fours for me," I demand. I'll show her exactly what type of man I am and how much I cherish her body. There's plenty of time later for baby talk. Much later. Tonight, I'm focusing on the pleasure side of making them.

CHAPTER TWENTY-NINE

LACEY

CURRENT DAY

A SENSE OF DÉJÀ VU WASHES OVER ME AS I STARE DOWN AT THE double blue lines in disbelief. How is this possible? We've been careful the entire time since our first encounter. How am I going to break the news to him, now?

Zach's in Atlanta finishing off the regular season against the Braves. He's been doing well since his return, and it looks as if the move to the bullpen has been pure genius. There's even talk about making him a closer sometime in the future.

Postseason starts next week, which means one month at the most to wait. But I'm dying to tell someone. This news is too huge to keep bottled inside. Zach's out of the equation, at least until baseball wraps up for the season, so I do the next best thing. I call Jocelyn.

"Hey, girl, what's up?" she greets me.

"I'm pregnant."

She begins to choke. "What!"

I really need to learn how to soften the blow.

"I thought you said you weren't? How is this possible?"

"I wasn't. But either I'm Fertile Myrtle, in definite need to be on some form of birth control, or Zach's super sperm is strong enough to break through condoms. Take your pick because I don't know."

"Jeez, girl. Quit freaking out. Have you told Zach yet?"

"No."

"What are you waiting for?"

"I plan to. Real soon. I'm just waiting for the baseball season to end. Since the Phillies are going to the playoffs, I want to wait. It's only a month at the most."

"That's understandable." She blows out a breath. "At least, it's not like last time. Zach will be there for you, and he'll be thrilled."

"I hope so."

I'm not as confident as Jocelyn. After Zach's near panic attack when he came back home and finally remembered he may have impregnated me, I don't think he's quite ready for the news. I can't take the risk of blowing his chance in the postseason.

Jocelyn's confidence comes in spades. She may have been shaken this past month and a half, but she's one strong woman. I wish I had half her courage.

I'm hoping the Phillies go all the way this year, but the selfish side of me can't wait for their season to end. I just hope he's as happy as I am. Either way, this should prove to be interesting.

CHAPTER THIRTY

LACEY

CURRENT DAY

OCTOBER BASEBALL AT CITIZENS BANK PARK CAN'T BE BEATEN. I turn and look at Zoe who's now bouncing in her seat. She's excited to see her daddy pitch. Chicago's in town, and it's the bottom of the eighth. We have a two-run lead. The problem? The series is tied, and it comes down to this game. Plus, the Chicago is having a helluva year which means Zach has inherited the bases loaded. Our saving grace? The Cubs haven't won a National League Championship Series title since 1945. Surely, this isn't their year. As far as Zach goes, moving to the bullpen has been a blessing thus far. The last few games he's been unhittable. I hope that continues through tonight.

"Come on, Zach." I lean forward in my seat and stare intently at the field. "You just need one out."

"Come on, Daddy," Zoe yells.

Zach steps to the mound to throw a practice pitch. His foot digs in. His fingers wrap around the ball, and he raises his hands in front of his face. Then it happens. That damn tic. My heartbeat literally skips before pounding as fast as the wings of a hummingbird.

"Oh no," I whisper. "*Please* be okay."

He throws the pitch, and I study his face. Other than him biting down on his lip, I don't see any other signs of pain. After a few more throws, he appears to be doing better, and I calm down somewhat.

The batter steps up to the plate. Zach sets up and throws the ball.

Strike one.

"Two more to go, baby," I yell.

"Two more," Zoe repeats my words.

I hold my breath at his windup. He throws, but I don't notice the hanging curve ball. I don't notice the ball popping off the bat nor the groans of the crowd. All I notice is Zach now currently holding his shoulder, biting back a scream.

I lose all sense of reality as every Cub player comes into score. I can't think as the trainer rushes to the field. With one simple look, they escort him to the dugout.

"Where they taking Daddy?"

Zoe's voice snaps me out of my trance, and I grab her hand. "Let's go find out."

I worm my way through the seats down to their dugout, hoping to obtain any information. Jax eyes me snaking my way to the side of the dugout and wastes no time to greet me.

"I'll try and find out what happened," he says.

"Get me back there to him, Jax."

"I'll see what I can do."

It feels like a lifetime passes when Jax makes it back out of the dugout.

"Go to the clubhouse door, and Bruno will let you in."

I hold a hand across my stomach and nod.

"Come on, Zoe. Let's go to Daddy."

"Is Daddy okay?"

"I don't know, sweetheart, but I sure hope so."

"Bruno?" I ask when we approach the guarded doors.

"Ma'am." The tall, burly guy nods. "What's your name?"

"Lacey. Lacey Pritchett."

He steps aside, and I grab hold of Zoe's hand and make my way through the door. I'm so upset the slip of my name doesn't faze me. Walking down the corridor, I stop in front of the locker room. With a deep breath, I swing the door open and march inside. Zach is sitting on an exam table. He raises his head, and his gaze meets mine.

I swallow hard as a pain squeezes my chest. His look is fearful, frightened. His eyes lower to take in Zoe's presence. The pain of regret flashes through his eyes, and I want to die. I hold my stomach again and fight back the scream on the tip of my tongue.

"Daddy!" Zoe breaks from my hand and races across the floor.

"Zoe, come back. Give Daddy space," I say as I dash ahead to catch her. The last thing I need is for us to be tossed out of the locker room.

"It's okay." Zach lowers his good arm on top of Zoe's head as she hugs his legs. "Daddy will be okay, sweetheart. It's okay."

His words are hollow, and I know he doesn't believe it.

"Let's get you to the hospital for the MRI. I'm not so positive this time around," the trainer says.

I stand next to Zach, and his fingers curl around my thigh.

"I'm so sorry. I'll figure something out to do."

His statement confuses me. He's not making sense. "What are you talking about?"

"Workwise. I'll figure something out to support us."

"Don't talk like that, Zach. You'll be fine." I turn to face him and place my hands on the sides of his cheeks. "No matter the circumstances, we'll be fine."

If only I knew how haunting those words could be.

CHAPTER THIRTY-ONE

ZACH

CURRENT DAY

"And the devastating loss for the Phillies as they drop their World Series bid by losing to the Cubs 4-2."

"Yes, Phil. The headlines have been the Cubs finally making the World Series, but the hanging question is: 'Is this a career-ending injury for the Cy Young Winner Zach Pritchett?'"

I turn the television off and groan. I let my team down. Four outs away from going to the World Series, and I fucking blow it for them.

I look over at Lacey and Zoe. The future I had for them is destroyed. I made her move to be with me, and now, I don't know how I'm going to support her.

"Hey," she says softly. "Whatever happens, we'll face it together."

I remain tight-lipped and glance away. I don't deserve her.

The doctor comes into the room, and the crestfallen expression tells me everything I need to know. I'm fucked.

Lacey's fingers tighten around my hand as he places the images of my shoulder on the light box. My career, my future, my new contract hangs in the wings and is reduced to a black-and-white image.

"Mr. Pritchett, what you seem to have is a tear in the rotator cuff."

I close my eyes as the doctor's words mesh together. He's speaking, but I'm no longer capable of hearing anything but white noise. My entire future has crashed around me.

I withdraw my hand from Lacey and reopen my eyes.

"If you want to proceed with surgery, we can schedule it for tomorrow."

Surgery? It seems I've missed a bit of information, but of course, I'll need surgery. It won't heal on its own. I nod. "Yes. The faster we get this corrected, the faster I can ... heal."

I almost said play again, but we all know the probability of that is slim to none. My gaze finds Lacey's. Her eyes are filled with sympathy. *Fuck.* I made her quit her job. For me. When I knew I may be having problems? I'm such a fucking prick. She deserves so much better than me.

"Great. I'll have the nurse schedule you, and I'll see you tomorrow."

"We'll get through this, Zach," Lacey reassures.

But that's all the words are. Senseless reassurance. I don't say anything. In fact, I remain in a quiet state the entire time while the nurse discusses the information, while the Coach gives his parting words, and during the entire ride home. When we enter the apartment, I head straight to my bedroom and slam the door, shutting out Lacey and Zoe and pretty much the entire world. All I want is to be left alone.

CHAPTER THIRTY-TWO

LACEY

CURRENT DAY

THE ANNOYING BUZZ OF MY PHONE ALARM JARS ME AWAKE AS A little arm drapes across my forearm. The sour taste in my mouth reminds me of the day we have ahead of us.

"Mommy, why are you in my room?"

I silence the noise and flip sides to face Zoe. She had crashed on the couch last night and didn't wake while I placed her in bed.

"Because, Snugglebug, I think Daddy needed some time alone last night."

"Because of his boo-boo?" Large inquisitive eyes stare back at me, and it takes great effort not to wince.

"Yeah, he's worried about his surgery. Maybe we shouldn't bother Daddy too much this morning. Okay?"

She nods and rolls back over. "I want to sleep a little more."

"Okay, but only for a little while." I rise and lean over to kiss her cheek. "I'll be back to get you."

All three of us have gotten into a routine here, and if I'm telling the truth, this comfortableness comes as a surprise. With Zach being single for so long, I'd worried about his adjustment to an instant family, regardless if said family already belonged to him. But last night, even a blind person could tell he needed space. Time to adjust to his potential loss. So, I left him alone. Admittedly, I'd thought he'd come back out to talk. He never did. Without knowing what else to do, I snuggled against Zoe once I placed her in bed.

I walk to the open kitchen and start my morning coffee. As soon as the smell wafts through the air, guilt overcomes me. Zach can't have anything to eat or drink, and he loves his morning coffee. Maybe I should've been more sensitive. We need to leave in forty-five minutes; perhaps I should've waited until we got to the hospital before I snuck in a cup.

After Zach went straight to the bedroom last night, he never emerged. He has to be starving. The click of his door echoes through the apartment, and I let out a breath. At least I don't have to wake him up.

"Morning," he mumbles when he walks over the kitchen table and sits.

"Morning." I fix my cup of coffee and lean against the countertop. Uneasiness refuses to leave. "Sorry, I probably should've waited. I hate drinking in front of you."

He runs his hand down his face and stares over at me. My stomach heaves from his haunting stare. Zach is full of life. Confident with a side of cockiness. I didn't expect rainbows to shoot out of his ass this morning, but this look of defeat scares me to my core.

"Where's Zoe?"

"In bed. I'm waking her up in a few minutes. She wanted to sleep a tad longer."

He nods and glances away, staring at nothing. I manage to finish my drink, but the churning in my stomach makes a second cup impossible. I turn off the coffeepot and walk over to the kitchen sink to rinse out my cup.

"I'll take a quick shower and get Zoe ready."

I wait a second for a response, but it never comes. Frustrated, I leave.

Zach remains quiet the entire trip to the hospital. While they prep him for surgery and up until the time they allow us to come wait with him, he doesn't say anything, other than to answer Zoe's questions. But she must've remembered me telling her to not bother her daddy, or maybe she can sense Zach's foul mood because she's abnormally quiet. He barely acknowledges Coach McFay or Jax when they come to offer support.

"The operating room nurse will be here in a few minutes to take you back," the pre-op nurse says as she pops her head through the door.

The stomach acid churns a little more as I watch her disappear.

"Lacey."

I turn toward Zach's pained expression and swallow.

"I want you to call Larry and beg for your job back. I should've never had Zoe and you come live with me. It wasn't right for me to be selfish."

"It wasn't right for you to want to be a family?" My stomach dips. The last thing I expected was him pushing me away.

He closes his eyes and shakes his head. "I knew my shoulder wasn't one hundred percent. I never should've pushed it, and I never should've asked you to give up a source of income. I'm useless now. I'll never be able to provide what you deserve. At least this way, you'll have a chance at meeting someone who could take care of you."

My dread turns to anger the longer he keeps talking, and my hand drapes protectively across my stomach.

"You listen here, Zach Pritchett. We don't get to choose who we love or don't love. And I don't know about you, but I love you. We *will* get through this! You, Zoe, and me. It'll be a hard road, no doubt. But whatever the outcome, we'll be fine."

"But I won't be able to provide—"

"Since when did my dreams consist of having an unprecedented amount of money?"

He clamps his jaw shut, not answering and staring anywhere but at me.

"Larry already has a contact for me here in Philly. In fact, I go for an interview next week."

His head snaps toward me, surprise replacing his pity party.

"Yeah, that's right. We'll be fine. I love you. That's all that matters."

"I love you too, Daddy. I don't want to go away."

Shit. I forgot Zoe was in the room. The panicked look returns to Zach. He must've forgotten she'd hear him as well.

"Sweetheart, I'd never leave you."

"You're my daddy, now. I don't want anyone else being my daddy."

For the first time since our goodbye in college, I witness tears well up in Zach's eyes, and I have to stave off my own.

"Zoe, I love you. Nobody else will ever be your daddy." His watery gaze flicks to mine. A beat of silence passes between us before he whispers, "I'm scared."

"Me too. But whatever the outcome, we'll be fine." I glance at Zoe and back to him. "Just as it should be."

"I love you." He reaches his hand out to me, and I lean in for the hug.

"I love—"

His lips find mine, cutting off my response. Every piece of emotion he's feeling is expressed in this kiss, and I feel it clear to my toes. A clearing of a throat interrupts, and we break away, eyes fixed on each other.

"I love you," he says, his confidence restored.

"I love you, too." I back away and grab hold of Zoe's hand.

"I love you, sweetheart," Zach says.

"I love you too, Daddy."

They wheel him down the corridor through the double doors. As the doors close, blocking off our view, I glance down at Zoe. "Let's say a prayer for Daddy."

She nods her head, and we walk out to the waiting room as

Zach's future now rests in the hands of the surgeons.

✖

THIS WAITING IS EXCRUCIATING. MY GAZE ROAMS ACROSS THE expanse of the waiting room, and I take in each anxious expression. There are other patients' family members here. Their loved ones' fate rests in the same boat as Zach's, but some are in far worse shape. The anxiousness, the worry. It's all displayed across their faces. In their conversations. Their silent prayers. I can't take much more.

Zach's coach is here along with the trainer, Jax, and AJ. No other team members are present. According to AJ, they wanted to be, and some did send Zach a text wishing him well, but there's no way this waiting room could house the entire team. I'm not surprised to see the lack of Zach's parents, but I was surprised that his older brother never showed. Zach never called him, but doesn't the guy own a television? The news may have been dominated by Chicago finally making it to the World Series, but they were still talking about Zach.

A guy in a sharply dressed suit slides next to Jax. He sets his expensive-looking leather briefcase by the seat next to him, never looking up from his phone. He types a few sentences before addressing Jax and Coach McFay. It isn't until he speaks that I realize who he is. Zach's agent, Darrel. His presence alone unsettles me. I don't need another reason to worry about this surgery. I know all too well that Zach wanted to extend his contract with the Phillies. I'm positive he wants to stay in this city. But now, his future in baseball may be over.

Zoe stirs beside me. "Mommy, how much longer will it be?"

"It's going to be a while yet, honey. Here, why don't you work on the picture you were coloring for Daddy." I open the coloring book to the page she started the other day.

"Daddy will feel better if I make this extra pretty. Daddy said he loves my drawings."

193

"Yes, he does." I run my fingers through her hair and glance up at Jax staring at us.

"He always loved you, you know."

This isn't the time nor the place for this discussion, but I love hearing the words nonetheless. Even though they make me sad.

"We wasted so much time," I say, trying to hide the sadness infiltrating my tone, but failing terribly.

"Yeah, but you have now." His gaze drops to Zoe. "I'm so sorry you went through everything alone."

"I figured you'd be mad at me. Especially since you're his best friend."

"Nah, I know how stubborn Zach was when he left you. I understand the position you were in." He scrunches his face. "Eh, I may have been part of the problem."

"What do you mean?"

"I may be the reason why Zach was with that girl."

"You didn't make him do anything, Jax. No one forced him into it."

"Yeah, but he kept whining the entire summer, and I sort of told him to go get"—he glances down at Zoe and cringes—"over you. I had no clue that you were going to show up. I feel awful."

Not near as awful as I felt. "Yeah, that hurt and I honestly thought that he used me."

"No, he loved you. Still does. I'm glad he finally came to his senses."

"Thanks, Jax. That means a lot to me."

And I meant that too. Jax is Zach's best friend. It makes things run smoother if everyone gets along. I open my mouth to speak but say nothing when Jax's face pales as if he's seen a ghost.

I follow his stare, and a smile crosses my face as my best friend Jocelyn walks through the door. I rise and give her a quick hug.

"Aunt Jocelyn," Zoe yells and runs over to hug her.

"Hey, sweetheart. I thought maybe you could keep me company." Jocelyn looks over at me. "And you may need a break?"

"Thank you," I mouth.

Her gaze falls on Jax, and her smile falters.

"Jax," she says in an unfriendly tone.

I quickly think back to when we were in college, scanning my memories to see when they would've interacted. But every memory has had Carl with her. Not once did Jocelyn and I ever hang with Zach and Jax. How do they know each other?

"It's been awhile."

I watch their interaction in awe. Evidently, I'm missing a crucial piece of information. One that I have every intention of finding out. Later. When my plate isn't so full.

Jocelyn grabs Zoe's hand, and they leave. Jax's gaze follows them on their way out. They still haven't returned when the nurse comes into the room. The coach, Zach's trainer, and I all stand when she motions for us to follow. We don't say a word as she leads us into a small room. We continue to remain silent as we settle into the chairs and wait for the doctor.

Each tick of the clock feels like hours passing until the surgeon finally waltzes through the door wearing a smile. A smile is a good sign. Right?

"I have some good news."

Relief floods my body from the best five-word arrangement that has ever fallen upon my ears.

"He had a partial tear that was able to be corrected through the scope. What this means is his recovery time will be less. There will be a lot of work involved on Zach's part, and I can't say he'll come back to his elite performance, but the probability exists that he'll still be able to pitch."

"Thank you so much, Doctor."

"He's going into recovery where he'll stay for another hour or so, then he'll go to his own room. Once he's there, you can see him. He'll be able to go home later today."

We shake the doctor's hand and return to the waiting room. I know there's a lot of work left to do, but at least Zach's outcome doesn't remain so bleak. And as good as everything sounds, I won't be able to fully relax until I see the whites of Zach's eyes.

CHAPTER THIRTY-THREE

ZACH

CURRENT DAY

IT WILL BE A LONG RECOVERY, BUT I'LL GLADLY TRADE THE HARD work involved over not receiving an offer at all. The relief I feel from knowing I'm not as injured as the surgeon first thought doesn't even compare to having Lacey and Zoe by my side. And to think, I almost told them to walk away. What the hell was I thinking? They're mine. An extension of me. I'll never let them go.

I'm about to be discharged, and Jocelyn just left with Zoe. I turn to Lacey and raise an eyebrow.

"So, Jocelyn and Jax were in the same room? How'd that go?"

Lacey's eyes widen. "What do you mean? Is there a history between them?"

"Yep. The beginning of Freshman year. How'd you think I was able to get information about you so easily from her back in college?"

"Oh my God. I thought you bribed her or something."

"Bribe? My looks and charm alone could've sealed the deal."

"You think, huh?" She tries to suppress her smile.

"Oh, yeah. I know."

She shakes her head. "I can see the surgeon restored your cockiness."

I laugh, but her face grows serious.

"How are you feeling?"

"Hurts like hell, but the pain meds help."

My agent peeks in the doorway. "Hey," he says.

"Darrel, did you bring me good news?"

After finding out about my outcome, he's been on the phone with the upper brass.

"They're offering a one-year contract contingent upon your performance, but I can push for a better deal. Or one with more money."

Coach McFay came through.

My agent's tone tells me I should take what the Phillies are offering. I'm no fool. I won't pass up their deal. The entire organization has been good to me straight out of college. My home is here, in this great city, and I don't wish to go anywhere else.

"Tell them I'll take the deal."

"You're positive. I really think I can get an extended time frame, but it'd come with a trade clause."

I glance at Lacey, and I've never been more positive in my life. "Yeah, I'll sign it. I don't plan on leaving." Some things are worth more than money. I have the offseason to recover plus part of spring training. I'll be sitting out for the first part of the season, but I plan on returning. Strong.

As soon as Darrel leaves, Lacey saunters over to me.

"Now, how do you feel?"

"Like I'm the luckiest man in the world."

"I think those drugs are doing you wonders. Perhaps you shouldn't make decisions affecting your career when you're high."

"Nah, I already know my answer. I'll prove to the Phillies how good I still am, and they'll offer me an extension. Or we'll decide to go somewhere else then."

"No more talk about sending me away."

"Fuck no. You're mine." I place my hand on top of hers and squeeze as much as the IV in my hand will let me. "I don't know what I ever did to deserve you. I've gotten a second chance and will never fuck it up again. You and Zoe belong with me. Always. I'm never letting you two go."

She bends down and plants a soft kiss on my lips.

"It's about time you realize what you have, Mr. Pritchett," she murmurs, a breath away. "And your speech would've been really sweet if you didn't say the word fuck twice."

My lips twitch. She's so fucking cute.

"Marry me."

"What?" She backs away and stares at me as if I lost my mind. "You *are* high."

"No, I'm not. Well, maybe a little." I shrug. "But I know what I want, and I want you. I want our family to be together as one. I want us all to have the same last name."

The smile that stretches across her face is the sexiest, cutest thing I've ever seen.

"When you come out of this drug-induced pain therapy regimen, I'm going to hold you to your words."

"Is that a yes?"

"That's most definitely a yes."

"Come here." I pull her arm, so she'll be at my level. "My breath is bad, but I want a kiss."

A chuckle escapes her beautiful mouth. My eyes drop to those full lips that have given me great pleasure throughout the years.

"Zach," she says through panted breaths.

"Yeah." I watch her mouth open and shut as my name rolls from her lips.

"We may need a bigger place."

"Mmm, okay." Anything this girl wants is hers. Although I have no idea why she'd bring this up now. Not when I want to taste her. "Anything you want, babe."

"Zach."

I force myself to look up at her eyes. Eyes that look half-frightened. *What the fuck?*

"We need a bigger place."

"You said that. I have nothing against finding a larger apartment."

"We need at least three bedrooms."

"Okay, if you want a guest—" My eyes widen as her words sink into my thick skull. The night I greedily took advantage of her outside the clubhouse in a dirty alley springs to mind. The sex was great but also without a condom. But she already denied being pregnant. My eyes dip to her abdomen. Wouldn't she be showing? Christ, that was months ago. "You're not pregnant, are you?"

She presses her lips together and nods. Tears spring to her eyes. I'm not sure if those are happy tears or I'm-scared-shitless tears.

"Come here," I order. I snake my arm around her neck and erase the gap between us. "Kiss me." She kisses me full on. When we break apart, I lean my forehead on hers. "I'm so fucking happy."

"You're not mad?"

"Hell no, babe. We'll get through this together. I need to get back in shape to help you out."

She laughs but then turns serious.

"I kept waiting to tell you. I wanted to tell you right as I found out, but you had to do your rehab stint. Then the playoffs. Then you got hurt. I'm sorry I told you at the hospital. I just couldn't wait any longer."

"Hey, calm down. I don't want you to stress our little bambino in there." I place my hand on her stomach area. "I can't believe there's a child growing inside you."

Her hand crosses over mine, and a silence descends upon us. I know what she's thinking. She's thinking about the regrets of me missing the first child. It still hurts, knowing I missed so much. But I'm done being upset. We moved forward, and I don't plan on regressing. Lacey is every part of my life now and will be forever.

"After I'm healed, we'll look for some venues to get married." I take her left hand and rub her ring finger. "We'll pick out a ring, too."

"I love you, Zach Pritchett."

The corner of my lip raises as I stare back at Lacey.

"I love you, Mrs. Lacey Pritchett."

EPILOGUE

ZACH

ONE YEAR LATER

My fingers grasp the baseball, and I run my thumb across the baby-soft leather and raised stitching. I love the contrast from smooth to rough. But more importantly, I love the power that comes with holding this baby in the palm of my hand. It all comes down to the next three outs.

The cheers seem muffled, as if I'm in a tunnel, as I scan the ballpark and absorb their excitement. There's a buzz in the air. A current that pulses through my veins. The time I've waited for my entire life has arrived—game seven of the World Series, top of the ninth with a two-run lead.

It doesn't get any better than this.

My gaze falls to the box seats that house my wife and beautiful daughter and son. Even though I can't see them, I know their watchful eyes are spying down on me in hopeful anticipation. A sense of pride swells inside me. This time last year, I didn't know if I'd ever play again, much less play for the Philadelphia Phillies. A team that had stuck by me my entire career, including my demise of last year. I lost our bidding for the World Series and let my team down. It took a lot of hard work and determination, but I managed to come back. With the starting rotation a thing of the past—an adjustment I made toward the end of last season—my talents are now best served in the closer position. Midway through this year, I garnered control over my cutter and curveball and have been untouchable ever since.

Three more outs.

What sweet redemption this could be. With this save, my future will be set, family secure, and a championship to top off the scene. Sweet redemption indeed.

I step to the rubber and place my left foot against the home plate side.

I stare into AJ's eyes. He gives me the signal, and I nod, set, and throw.

Fastball, up and high.

Strike one.

The next pitch gets fouled off.

Strike two.

I adjust and throw my cutter.

Strike three. Out number one.

AJ throws the ball back to me, and I rub the ball with my thumb again.

This next batter likes to swing at anything high and away. Every player has a pattern they follow. Some sort of weakness. The coaches can tell them to lay off certain pitches until they're blue in the face. But these guys can be stubborn. When the ball appears hittable, they swing, essentially striking out. It's that occasional hit when they connect that feeds their addiction to keep swinging.

As he steps to the plate, I know exactly the pitch I'll be throwing. High heat, away.

Smack.

Shit, he connected. I watch the ball pop out to right field. Rodriguez runs in, and I think the ball will drop, but he makes a leaping dive and somehow comes up with the ball in his glove.

Out number two.

I point to Rodriguez with a you're-the-man salute. Damn, he saved our ass.

Refocusing on the next batter, I stare at my catcher as he flashes my new signs.

With a quick two strikes, AJ sets up and wiggles two fingers. Knuckle curveball. The same pitch that ended our World Series run last year. I shake him off, but he signals the same sign. *Shit. I've got this.*

Not everyone is deserving of a second chance, and I'm not saying I am. But I got one anyway with family *and* a career. And you can bet your sweet ass, I damn sure won't waste it. How many chances does a guy get at becoming a second-chance hero in more ways than one? *I've got this.*

Placing my middle finger along the bottom seam and thumb across the back seam, I tuck my index finger under. *I've got this.* I windup, my knuckle points to my target, and I throw. The batter smacks the ball to the shortstop, Jax. He scoops the ball, double pumps, and throws to first base.

Holy shit! We won!

I throw my arms up and let out a yell. A roar ruffles through the stadium, and I turn to Jax who's running to me, arms spread wide.

"Yeah! You did it!" he yells, wrapping his arms around me.

The next thing I know, I'm tackled by a horde of teammates. Jumping. Shouting. Congratulating.

When they break away from me, I scan the field and search for my family. I shouldn't have to wait long before they're allowed to join us.

I'm interrupted by the media while the lady drills me with a few questions. Gonzalez comes from behind and lifts me in the air, officially ending my interview. With a few more fist bumps and hugs from teammates and congratulations from the opposing team, the Angels, I see my family running toward me. Finally!

"You did it," Lacey says with tears streaming down her eyes.

"Daddy, you're number one!" Zoe says as I reach down to pick her up.

Lacey juggles our son on her hip as we embrace in a family group hug. I was wrong before. This moment right here ... yeah, life doesn't get any better than this.

DON'T WANT TO MISS BAD BOY, JAX CARRIGAN, IN SWING FOR The Fences? Just flip the page for more details.

JOIN KIMBERLY READNOUR'S NEWSLETTER

Don't want to miss any new releases? Go to website www.kimber-lyreadnour.com and join my newsletter to receive updates, and as a bonus, you will receive a free novella for your enjoyment. Enjoy!

Read the first chapter of Swing For The Fences now! Just flip to the next page.

SWING FOR THE FENCES CHAPTER ONE

JAX

CURRENT DAY

The gravel crunches under my feet as each step brings me closer to my impending doom. *Great.* Now I sound like my roommate's overdramatic sister. Regardless, I work the coins deep inside my coat pocket. That moment—the one when I swallow the bitterness and pretend everything is fine—has arrived, and I still don't want to face the inevitable. Face *her*. Damn, I knew she would be here, so I shouldn't feel so unprepared.

Our team is coming off the high of winning the World Series. To keep the celebration going, Zach, my best bud and star closer, has thrown together this outdoor get-together—the team's last hooray before we split for winter break.

"Jax, my man. When did you get here?" Drake, our rookie backup catcher, cuts across the grass and impedes my progress.

I sneak a glance at the beautiful brunette cruising the buffet table. A pang of remorse tightens my chest, and bitterness leaves a bad taste in the back of my throat.

"Just now. I was running late." I leave out the *intentionally* part. Shit, I almost bailed, but Zach would kick my ass if I didn't show.

Well, he'd try, but I wouldn't let that happen. His multimillion-dollar pitching arm could get hurt, and that is the last thing we want.

"Nah, it's all good. They just set out the food." He lifts his full plate, and my gaze strays to the brunette again. Her feet carry her across the stamped concrete patio to the round firepit on the far side.

With each step she takes, her hair sways in the light breeze but not as much as her curvy hips. When I knew her, she was skinny with no meat on her. Guess that's what having three kids does to a woman's body. I'm definitely not complaining. Her new figure makes me want to swallow my tongue so I don't drool like a fucking caveman.

Drake nudges his chin in the direction I'm staring. "That hot piece of ass cooked most of it."

"Her name is Jocelyn." I clench the coins trapped in my fingers and try to keep my tone even. Drake raises an eyebrow at me, but I remain stoic.

"Hey, bro. Just sayin' I'd tap that even though it's cougar style."

Jesus, this kid doesn't know when to shut up. If anyone is in line for an ass-kicking, it's him.

"She's twenty-eight. Same age as me." I don't bother disguising the disdain in my voice.

"Like I said, cougar. Straight-up hot." He slaps me on the shoulder and reins in his tone. "Get some food, old man. You're grouchy."

"Fucking rookie," I mumble and stalk toward the tables. I'll fill my plate and then go join her. Better to get this awkwardness over with. The sooner the air clears between us, the quicker this nagging guilt can leave.

During an interview once, a journalist asked me what my biggest regret in life was. Who asks that? It's so personal. My brain scrambled to come up with a lie. The truth? I'll never admit that out loud. Uh-uh. There isn't any way I want the entire nation knowing my biggest regret was not being able to hold on to

Jocelyn Kennedy. She slipped through my fingers like a misfielded routine ground ball.

I grab a plate and scan the food. The heap of pulled pork looks surprisingly appetizing. My mouth waters as I pile the barbecue onto my plate. A few more scoops and my bases are loaded. Jesus, this is a lot of grub.

"Thought maybe you were going to pull another disappearing act." Zach pulls up next to me with his son draped over his shoulder. Poor kid looks worn out.

"I had my reasons for missing your wedding. You know that." I balance the plate and grab the utensils, avoiding eye contact.

Zach and Lacey's wedding was a small, private affair and one I hated to miss. Zach's been my friend since freshman year, and we've been teammates for almost the same amount of time. There was only one reason I didn't want to be there, and that would be the five-six bombshell currently sitting by the fire.

Zach follows my gaze. "Sorry, I didn't mean our wedding. I meant the other times you've conveniently copped out."

"Oh." Maybe my remorse is getting to me more than I thought.

"You going to talk to her this time?"

"Yeah, I better get it over with."

"It's been over ten years, man. I'm sure she's over your split."

"No shit, dickhead." She's been married and divorced since we broke up—no way she's still hung up on me. That's not the concern. The bigger question is, am I still hung up on her?

"Watch it. You don't want Lacey to hear you swearing around Tommy." He pats his kid on the back, but the little guy is out cold. "She's got a mean backhand slap."

I laugh. "Wife troubles?"

"Ha! You wish you had my problems."

Yeah, I do, sometimes.

Ever since Zach married Lacey, I've seen slight changes in him. He's happier. Content. They're fucking perfect for each other despite the rough and bumpy road they took.

I don't see myself as the settling-down type, but witnessing how happy they are leaves room for unwelcome thoughts. Ones that have no place in my bachelor's brain. But it doesn't matter because any type of relationship, short- or long-term, can't happen until I take care of the past. Purge my guilt. Flush all regrets. My gaze strays back to Jocelyn. Our championship logo brands the hoodie she's wearing and makes me think of the time she stayed in my dorm wearing nothing but *my* jersey and her damn smile that lit the entire shoebox of a room.

"Go talk to her. But good luck—she's a little salty since her divorce. Not that I blame her, but..."

"Thanks." I wink. "Think I got it covered."

"Okay then." He half-grins at my cockiness as if there's some hidden secret I'm not privy to. "I'm going to put this little guy to bed. Grab a beer. We'll catch up later." As an afterthought, he adds, "And lighten up, we just won the World Series."

A smile ghosts my lips for the first time this evening as Zach weaves his way through the crowd. I suck in a breath and stalk toward the firepit.

"Hey, stranger," I say as I approach.

Those chestnut eyes peer up at me, and my chest squeezes. Whenever Jocelyn looked at me, her gaze always held a brightness. An innocence that glowed. It was one of her best qualities. But not now. Sadness has replaced the luster of the woman in front of me. Fucking Carl. He killed the piece of her I treasured most. It's bad enough New York beat the southern accent out of her, but he didn't have to squash her best attributes.

"Jax." The sharp tone in her acknowledgment crawls over my skin, and I now want to drop-kick Carl. This aggressive vibe taking hold of me needs to leave. Inhaling some courage, I scoot the empty patio chair beside her and settle into it.

"The food smells great. Heard I have you to thank."

She turns back toward the fire. The firelight dances on her pale skin, illuminating her high cheekbones and slender neck. She really is a "hot piece of ass," as Drake puts it, but it isn't her looks that drew me to her in the first place. That's just a bonus. It's the clumsy imperfections, like the smudge of barbecue sauce on the side of her mouth, that I find adorable.

"I helped Lacey out." She studies the flames as she waves me off. "No biggie."

I press my lips together to suppress a grin. Same Jocelyn. Always putting others in front of herself. But this spread—pulled pork barbecue, some potato mixture, corn, and I don't even know what to call this vegetable salad thing—isn't anything to brush off. I take a bite of the questionable veggie mix and moan. It's fucking fantastic.

"You never give yourself enough credit. This is—" I chew a few times and swallow. "This is great."

She shrugs and doesn't say anything else.

I eat a few more bites because it tastes that good and I'm starving. Unable to stop myself, I steal glances at her while chewing. She stares into the flames, but I can't decipher her thoughts. Dark, haunted. Is this how she looked after our split? I somehow don't think so, considering she and Carl became an item right away. Toss in their five-year marriage, which produced three kids, and our breakup doesn't compare. The bitterness squeezes my chest again. I bet my World Series ring our split affected me more than her.

"I'm sorry to hear about your divorce." I may as well slap my cards on the table and get this awkwardness over with. The last thing I want to do is bring up her pain caused by another guy, but it's a dick move if I don't mention it.

Admittedly, when Zach told me what happened, the news ignited a tiny spark of hope. I thought I'd lost my one and only chance with Jocelyn our freshman year in college after she broke up with me, but I don't want my hope to be at her expense. I hate seeing her hurt. And she's been hurting for the past year.

"Thanks, it happens." Her dry tone slices through me, but when her gaze cuts back to me, I'm practically gutted. "You know he cheated on me, right?"

My throat becomes thick as I try swallowing a helluva lot more than food. I nod, not saying a word.

"I must be the type of girl everyone wants to cheat on." Her chin tilts up, mouth set as if she's trying to be strong. She could pull it off if I didn't already know her. She can't hide the emotions in her eyes. They've always spoken the truth, and right now, they scream of her pain.

I place the plate on the ground and lean closer to her, staying far enough away that we don't touch. "That's not true."

"Isn't it?"

"No." As the hard lines in her expression soften, I add, "Anyone who cheated on you is a damn fool."

She shakes her head and turns away. "Your words are hardly believable."

"Maybe, but I speak the truth." I sneak a glance at her as she continues to watch the flames. I should be a gentleman and tell her about the sauce on her face, but the tiny flaw keeps me grounded. What I prefer is a different type of sauce placed there. *Shit.* With everything she's dealt with this past year, my mind should stay away from any sexual thoughts when it comes to her.

"How're the kids?" I ask, switching gears.

A flicker of light dances in her eyes, and for a moment, I'm taken back to our freshman year. Pre-breakup, pre-marriage.

"They're...adjusting, but otherwise good." She lets out a tiny sigh, and just like that, the old Jocelyn is gone. "I can't believe that bastard fooled me all these years."

Fuck, I don't know what to say. Carl's an idiot. Yeah, I'll go with that, so I say it out loud.

She nods and then turns to me. "Why are all guys idiots?"

I don't know, but I don't say *that* aloud. Instead, I say something even stupider. "Come on. I wasn't that much of an idiot, was I? Or maybe I was—you fell in love awfully fast after our breakup."

As the words leave my mouth, regret slams back into me. But damn it, she was with him just six short weeks after our split. She ended up marrying the bastard for Christ's sake.

"Yeah?" She raises her eyebrows, challenging me. "And look where that landed me."

This reunion isn't going as well as I hoped. Before I can redeem myself, Drake crashes the conversation.

"Hey, is your roommate's sexy-ass sister here?"

"You mean Cara? I have no idea." My flat tone should have been an indicator for him to go away, but the pesky rookie doesn't know boundaries. "You shouldn't be looking for her anyway. Teammates' sisters are off-limits."

"Oh, come on, that girl oozes sex. Don't tell me you've never hit that."

Jocelyn bristles beside me, and I press my fisted hands into my thigh.

"Dude, have some respect." I gesture toward the lady present in case he isn't smart enough to figure out why.

Drake glances sideways to Jocelyn and then back to me. A knowing smile tugs at his mouth as he nods. "Okay, I see. I'll leave you two alone."

I blow out a breath and turn to Jocelyn. "Sorry, not all guys are assholes."

Her indifferent laugh doesn't go unnoticed, and from the way her gaze goes cold, I know she's thinking about our split again. Or maybe her and Carl's split. I don't know. What I did to her back then was a dickish move. Maybe we *are* all assholes.

"Present company excluded." I may as well own up to my actions.

She turns to me and pauses for a moment. A tiny glimpse of the girl I once knew makes another brief appearance. "You did have your moments. Good ones I mean."

We did, and we were good together. That's why I regret losing her.

I'm not sure what comes over me. Nostalgia? Compelled by her good looks? Some voodoo love potion hexing the food? I don't know, but my next words fly out before I can stop them. "We could give it another go."

Her lips part in shock, but those eyes tell a different story. Her pupils dilate with want, and that spark of interest is all I need to go after what I really want—Jocelyn, in my arms where she belongs.

"We can't. We... No. That's a bad idea."

"Why?"

Her jaw drops and then closes. Before she can answer, I lean in next to her ear. The apple scent from her hair overrides the camp-fire smell and makes me want to strip her clothes off and taste her. Even though I'm able to restrain myself from touching her, I'm not in control of my mouth.

"You know damn well how good we can be together." My voice comes across gruffer than I intend, but the hitch in her breath fuels me on. "Mmm, I'd lick that barbecue smudge off your cheek, but I don't think we're quite there. *Yet.*"

Her eyes widen as she raises a hand to the left side of her face.

"Other side, babe."

Her hair brushes the side of my cheek as I stand and leave with her staring after me. It only took a five-minute conversation to transport me back to college, when the most important things in my life were baseball and Jocelyn. The deets need to be worked out, but I guarantee one thing—Jocelyn Kennedy will be mine again. Bitter breakup or not.

ALSO BY KIMBERLY READNOUR

Bad Boys Redemption Series
Second Chance Hero
Swing For The Fences (6-20-2018)
Bottom of the Ninth (Summer 2018)

An *Unforeseen Destiny* Series:
Impossible Love

The *Mystical Encounter* Series:
Visions
Deceptions
Vanished

ACKNOWLEDGMENTS

First off, I want to say thanks to you, the reader, who took the time to read my work. I appreciate taking time out of your busy schedule to read my vision of a baseball romance.

Many don't know me, but if you've ever gone to my Facebook profile and clicked on the pictures, you would soon learn that I am a huge, Huge, HUGE Cub's fan. So you can imagine what kind of year I had with the Cubs winning the World Series. I was so thrilled because, honestly, I didn't think it would ever happen. So, what does that have to do with this book? It inspired me to write a sports romance book. Why? I couldn't tell you other than my love for baseball and love for romance. Somehow between the combination of the two, the series was born. I can't wait to share with you the rest of the stories.

Once again, thanks to my critique partners and beta readers! You people are the best at keeping me focused and keeping my voice young. Your insights are always spot on!

Thanks to all of my editors, from the developmental stage, content stage, and through to the proofreading stage. Each and every one of you is invaluable, and I can't thank you enough for helping me put out the cleanest manuscript possible.

ABOUT THE AUTHOR

Kimberly Readnour lives in the Midwest with her husband, two children, and a very fluffy cat.

Visions, book one of the Mystical Encounters Series, is a #1 Amazon Kindle bestseller and a 2015 Readers' Favorite book award finalist. Her series, the Mystical Encounters, has spent many weeks on the Amazon's teen and young adult's mysteries and thrillers bestseller's lists.

Kimberly worked as a Registered Nurse for fifteen years before hanging-up her stethoscope. When she isn't running her own business, you can find her tucked away writing.

Contact me at:
kimberlyreadnour.com
kimberly@kimberlyreadnour.com